love & liability

Also by Linda Cassidy Lewis

Bay of Dreams Series

The Brevity of Roses
An Illusion of Trust

High Tea & Flip-Flops Series

High Tea & Flip-Flops
Love & Liability
Open & Honest (Sometimes)

Edgewater Love Series
Building Love
Midnight Love

love & liability

A High Tea & Flip-Flops Novel

Linda Cassidy Lewis

-246-
Two-Four-Six Publishing

Cover design: Studioelle

For Robert, Michael, Joseph, and Daniel.
My most rewarding creations ever.

one

Want to know how pathetic my life is? I'm twenty-four years old and living with my fiancé—in my mother's house. And what's worse is that they're both happy with this situation. You're probably thinking Jeremy's some Peter Pan type, but that's not him at all. He was a lawyer in London and owned his own condo and stuff before he moved here to California to write romance novels. Seriously.

So, here we are. And right now, Jeremy's just chilling on the sofa beside me while we're waiting for dinner. He and Mom are watching BBC World News, but my mind's on something else. I'm trying to decide if I should change the purple underlayer of my hair to blue or dye the blonde top layer purple too.

But as distracted as I am, my ears perk up at that little sigh my mom gives when she's about to say something important.

"You know, dear," she says to Jeremy, "if your family lived here, Chelsea and I would have already gotten to know them."

Uh-oh, I have a bad feeling I know what she's leading up to.

"Yes, … I suppose you would have." He gives me a side-ways glance.

"But," she says, "it's not like London is on another planet."

"Geographically that's true, but in some ways …" Because his British politeness has kicked in, he's smiling at her, but he's squeezing my hand. Hard.

It won't work, but I have to react to his plea for me to do something to divert her. "Mom, shouldn't you check on dinner?"

She frowns at me. "You go check it, Chelsea. I'm discussing something with Jeremy."

His crushing grip on my hand says he's also figured out what she's leading up to and he might strangle me if I leave him alone to fend off this conversation.

"So." Mom pauses, ready to move in for the kill. "I was thinking—"

"Whatever it is smells delicious, Marie."

My pretty, blonde mother is usually unflappable, smiling through situations that frustrate or anger me. My dad called her his sweet petite. But right now her frown at both of us borders on a glare. How could Jeremy not have learned by now that he can't derail her train of thought?

"As I was trying to say, I've given this a lot of thought, and I think it's past time you introduced us to your family. So I'd like for us to plan a trip to London."

The jolt of alarm that proposal gives him results in serious pain in my hand, and I elbow his ribs to make him let loose. There's no way in hell Jeremy will agree to that trip.

"That's a good idea, Marie." He flashes his irresistible grin. "I'll speak to my parents about it."

"Wonderful." She stands and smooths her perfectly styled hair and brushes at her spotless clothes as if she'd just wrestled that answer out of him—literally. "I'd better go check on dinner."

My mouth is still hanging open at Jeremy's response, but as soon as she leaves the room, he's on his feet and pulling me down the hall and into our bedroom.

"I see no point in traveling to London," he says when I shut the door behind us. "It's certainly not an expense we can afford on top of the wedding."

"Mom knows that. If she suggested the trip, it's because she's offering to pay for it. She wants to go with us."

That shuts his mouth but only for a second. "Well, that's impossible because we are not going."

"Well … maybe we should. I think it's time."

"Since when?"

"Since … oh, we both knew it was inevitable."

"But they—" His mouth snaps shut.

"They what?" Ohmygod. "They don't want to meet me?"

"It's not that." He rubs his hands down his face. "They don't know we're engaged."

"Oh yeah."

"And, obviously, you were fine with that."

"I never said that."

He gestures as if I've proven his point. "You never mentioned it at all. Did you ask if I'd told them or how they responded? No. And we both know why."

The look in his eyes dares me to disagree, but I can't. Knowing who they'd already chosen for Jeremy to marry makes me pretty sure they won't be all that thrilled with his choice.

"Yeah. Okay. I avoided the subject. But I've been thinking about it lately. I have to be introduced to them. And don't you think it's going to be way more awkward for everyone if we meet for the first time at the wedding?"

"Problem solved." He looks away. "They won't be at the wedding."

"Wait, what? They couldn't have said they won't come if they don't even know—"

"They won't be invited."

"Like hell."

He crosses his arms. "I said they will not be invited. Discussion. Over."

"Hey, Mr. High Tea, send Jeremy back."

There goes his right eyebrow, arching halfway to his hairline. "Your attempt at wit is not in your favor, Flip-Flops."

"And your attempt at pretending you're the boss in this relationship is hilarious." (Oh yeah, he's learned a lot about me in the last few months too.)

He sighs and lets his arms drop to his sides. "Chelsea, please. Why would you want to meet people who have no interest in me and hence no interest in the woman I'm going to marry? The only family I care about is my sister. You may invite Laura to the wedding. And my uncle."

"We're inviting your whole family to the wedding, Jeremy. Even your brother."

"No. We. Are. Not."

"That's ridiculous!"

"I beg your pardon," he says. "Have I no say in this at all?"

"No matter what problems you had with your family in the past, they have to be invited."

"Is that a law in your country?"

"It's custom, smart-ass. I bet it's custom in England too. And since when is this not your country—at least by half?" (Jeremy's parents are British citizens, but he was born in Massachusetts, so he has dual citizenship.)

He gives me that squinty-eyed thing he does when I prove him wrong, so I give him my you-can't-resist-me pout and back him up toward the bed.

"Come on, tall, dark, and handsome. We can't have the groom's side empty of guests."

"Sides," he mutters. And then he pulls me down on the bed. Which is, of course, the exact minute my mom calls us to dinner. Jeremy flies off the bed, pulling me along with him. "We will resume that activity as soon as possible."

"Reason number seven hundred and fifty-six why we shouldn't be living with my—"

"Yes, yes, I know." And he's out the door.

Dinner is pot roast, Jeremy's favorite. My mom treats him like a king. You'd think she was his mother, not mine. But I'm not really jealous because from what I understand Jeremy's mother never treated him like that. And to be honest, he treats us both like queens, so it's all good.

When the royal family is all seated, I start the conversation to divert my mom from mentioning the London trip again. "Gabi is driving me crazy with the wedding planning."

My mother pats my hand. "Well, sweetie, you should be glad she's doing that."

"Why?"

She and Jeremy exchange a look.

"You know how you are," she says.

"What do you mean how I am?"

With another look, she passes the question to Jeremy.

"Well …" He rearranges his napkin. "You …" He spaces the salt and pepper shakers one inch apart. (I could probably verify that with a ruler.) He gives me a hesitant smile. "Sometimes … you're a bit lax with details."

"Seriously? You trust me with the details in our writing. You've even praised me for catching your continuity errors."

"Oh. Yes, of course, in our writing …" He looks to my mom for help, but she only shrugs and forks a chunk of potato into her mouth.

"But?" I prompt.

"But … in real life …"

I grab a dinner roll and bounce it off his forehead. He and my mom sigh and slowly shake their heads. In tandem. That right there is reason number seven hundred and fifty-seven why we shouldn't be living here. I swear, the first time he pats my hand and calls me sweetie, I'll punch him.

"If I'm so bad at it, then you can take care of the wedding details."

"And deprive Gabi of the pleasure?"

He's right about that. Gabi planned her elaborate wedding for years and then scrapped the whole idea when she got pregnant. She tried to pretend the small ceremony in her mother's house was perfect, and it was sweet and beautiful, but I'm her best friend; she couldn't fool me. It wasn't anything like she'd described to me—in never-ending detail—throughout our high school and college years. Except for the groom. She was totally happy that it was Matt standing beside her and saying, "I do." He's gorgeous and smart and hardworking and the exactly right guy for Gabi.

Anyway.

I feel I owe her the joy of planning my wedding. And to be honest, I know she'll make the best decisions. It's going to be a beach wedding—that's about the extent of my planning ideas.

"You're right," I say. "Gabi's in her element. And I have other things to worry about."

Jeremy looks up from his plate. "Like what?"

"Like what comes after the book we're writing now. We're starting a new series, right?"

He chews for a moment. "If you say so."

"Me? They're your books."

He frowns. "I don't think of them as mine at all."

"Okay, they're ours. But if we start a new series, we'll have to have a new theme. What will it be?"

"Romantic suspense might be nice," my mom says.

Jeremy grins at me. "There you go."

I blink. Twice. "You've never once mentioned us writing romantic suspense."

"Does it sell well, Marie?"

My mother doesn't blink. "Definitely."

Like she would know. She's never studied the romance book market in her life. Not that she's wrong.

Jeremy's resumed eating, so I direct my next question to his bent head. "Have you written any kind of suspense before?"

He lifts his head but looks toward my mom. "This dinner is delicious … as always."

I huff. "Jeremy?"

"What have you made us for dessert, Marie?"

"Pecan pie."

His eyes light up. It's one of his favorites. Of course.

I snap my fingers. "Hel-lo."

The face he turns toward me is blank with innocence. "Yes, short, blonde, and gorgeous?"

"We were talking about our next—"

"Please"—Jeremy cuts another bite of roast—"let's not discuss business over this excellent dinner."

"Since when do we not discuss business at dinner?"

Both of them smile at me.

Reason number …

I push Jeremy's shoulder.

"What? What?"

"You're snoring."

He mumbles something and turns on his side.

I can't get to sleep. I've been lying here freaking out. It probably doesn't seem like it, after my dinner roll throwing, but I'm trying hard to master this adulting thing. It doesn't help that Jeremy acts more than just three years older than me. I'm just afraid I'm never going to get the hang of being a real adult.

I mean, right now Jeremy thinks it's cute when I do stupid things like throwing bread at him. Or when I say something totally dumb or inappropriate—ohmygod, I swear sometimes my brain is not connected to my mouth. Just last month when Jeremy and I went out to dinner with Mom and one of her friends, who happens to be a priest, I totally freaked the man out. I can't help groaning now as it all comes back to me.

"I'm so happy you invited me out for dinner tonight, Marie," Father Jacobs said. "I don't get out as much as I used to since I retired." He chuckled. "Not many people care to spend their evening with an old priest."

"Oh, nonsense," my mom said, "I've always enjoyed your company."

She didn't bother telling him he's not old since he's about ninety, which isn't young no matter how you look at it.

"When I called," she said, "your housekeeper told me you were at war over a house repair. What was that about?"

"My gutters." For a moment, he closed his eyes and hung his head, shaking it slowly. "I hired someone to repair a section, but he said it would have to be replaced. I agreed to that and then left for a church meeting. When I came home, two hours later, I found out he'd torn down all the guttering and hauled it away. I ended up being charged for a whole new gutter system."

"That's fucked up," I said.

To a priest.

To an old priest.

I wanted to die. Mom looked like someone had smacked her in the face. Jeremy was about to bust a gut from trying not to laugh. Father Jacobs paled, smiled weakly, and hailed our waiter with a shaky hand.

He ordered another bottle of wine, which I'm pretty sure he drank the most of.

Anyway.

If I were a responsible adult, I wouldn't do stuff like that, right?

For now, Jeremy takes it in stride when I do and say those kinds of things. But sooner or later, they'll start annoying him. They won't be funny anymore. So I have to change. Being Chelsea Cole has become a liability. I have to learn to act like an adult before I become Chelsea Pearce.

In four months.

And what about after that? My mom's already hinting

about being a grandmother. How could she wish any child to have me for a mother? Oh, right, in her scenario we'd all be living with her forever, so she'd be taking care of the baby. Or at least making sure I didn't psychologically scar it for life.

But don't forget that details thing Jeremy and Mom made clear I suck at. There's a bazillion details to keep track of as a mother. What if I forgot to feed my baby? No, bad example —I'm pretty sure they let you know when they're hungry. But I could forget other important things. I could forget I have a baby. What if the baby was sleeping, and I just totally spaced and left the house? I might be gone for hours.

No. I'm not responsible enough to be a mother.

I'm not responsible enough to be a wife.

Sometimes I wonder if I'm even responsible enough to be a human.

♥ ♥ ♥

Two days later, Jeremy and I are in the kitchen cleaning up after dinner. Until his lease ran out, we lived in his place at the Ocean View Luxury (not) Apartments. I wanted us to rent another apartment then, but Jeremy, in uncharacteristic frugality, voted to accept my mom's offer of sharing her house —"just until your finances stabilize." The problem is, as far as she's concerned, our finances will never be stable.

Anyway.

Part of the deal we have with her is a division of chores. When she cooks, we clean up the kitchen, which usually means that Jeremy fills the dishwasher, and I hand-wash anything that won't fit or can't go in there. But tonight he's got sex on his mind, so he keeps stopping to kiss me or feel me up.

"Give it a rest, Jeremy, and get your job done."

He grimaces and lays a hand over his heart. "Thy rejection hurts."

"Yeah? Well, if we had our own—"

He clears his throat in a warning sort of way, and when I turn to give him a dirty look, I see my mom crossing the kitchen. But she keeps moving and goes out the door to the garage. I presume she's going to her home office. After my dad died, Mom walled in what used to be his workshop area of the garage and converted it. She claims it's because the room has a door to the outside for her accounting business clients to use. I think it's because she feels closer to my father there.

"Looks like she'll be busy with work for a while," Jeremy says. Knowing exactly how sexy he looks to me with his shiny dark hair around his shoulders, he gazes deep into my eyes as he pulls the band off his ponytail and shakes his hair free.

"Oh, you are so obvious."

"Am I?" He steps behind me and slides his hands up under the front of my shirt.

"We are not doing anything here."

"Aren't we?" he whispers, his breath hot in my ear as he cups my breasts.

I turn to push him away, but he's quicker. He has my jeans unzipped and pushed halfway down my thighs when he's startled by the sound of the door from the garage opening. He jumps away from me so fast that I fall to my knees.

Mom glances at us and blushes hard. Looking like every ounce of her blood is pooled in her face, she pauses for only a second before stumbling past us with her hands held out like a blind woman making her way across an unfamiliar room.

I don't move. I just look up at Jeremy. His eyes are closed. "Jeremy."

"I know. I know," he mutters. "Reason number ... whatever."

"Can we finish the clean up now?"

He opens his eyes and gives me a hand up. "And then what?"

"Seriously?"

"I mean," he says, furiously finger combing his hair back into a tail, "we can't just walk into the living room and watch TV with her like nothing happened."

"She'll never mention it."

"Of course she won't. That's almost worse."

"You could tell her you'll start sleeping in our office." When he looks like he's actually considering that, I kick his foot. "That was a joke."

"Right. Well, when we're done here, I think I'll go for a drive."

Sigh. "I'll go with you."

"And allow your mother to watch Grey's Anatomy without you?"

"Okay then, we'll talk when you get back."

He shuts the dishwasher and grabs a towel to start drying the pans. "Talk?"

"It's been two days. We need to have another discussion about the London trip."

His face is blank, but I know his mind isn't. He's trying to decide whether to argue or keep his mouth shut. I wash and rinse and wait. When I finish and pull the plug, he hands me the towel.

"I'll be back," he says.

By the time I've dried the last few items, he's not back, so

I turn off the light and head to our bedroom. He's not there. He's not in our office either. I go to the living room.

"Mom, have you seen Jeremy?"

"No, but I heard the front door close while I was on the phone. Didn't you know he was going out?"

"Yeah. Sure. I just didn't know when." So that's the game he's playing.

She pats the sofa cushion next to her. "Come sit with me, sweetie. The show's about to start."

As the opening begins, I slip my phone out of my pocket and text him.

You can't avoid me forever, dude.

He doesn't respond.

two

When Jeremy wakes and heads to the bathroom, I'm awake but lying in bed with my eyes closed. The thought of meeting his parents scares the hell out of me, but I have to do it. I *have* to. That's the grown-up thing to do. Adults face what they fear, right? But how am I going to convince Jeremy to agree?

When he turns the shower on, I get out of bed. He doesn't hear me slip into the bathroom because he's singing. (That's a talent I didn't know he had until we moved in together.) I quickly brush my teeth. Then I strip and join him. He's always ready for sex in the morning.

"Well, hello there," he says.

"I just wanted to show you what you missed last night by"—I mime quotes—"driving around for hours."

He looks me up and down, turning me around. "Hmm, looks like I was a stupid git to pass up a chance to do this." He backs me against the shower wall and lifts me so my legs can circle his hips.

This is one of those instances when I'm happy about our

height difference. And for his strong arms and legs. And for hot morning showers with a sexy man.

Oh. Oh. Ohhhhh.

The idea of talking to him about the London trip floats right out of my mind.

As usual after breakfast, Jeremy and I go to our office. We don't have to leave the house to do that. This is a typical California ranch style: a four-bedroom, two-and-a-half bath one-level house with attached garage. When we moved in with Mom, she tried to give us the master bedroom, but we refused —on my part because I hoped we'd be here less than a week before Jeremy decided we needed more privacy. The joke's on me. We've lived here for *six* weeks already.

Anyway.

Jeremy and I took over the next largest bedroom. (Not my former room because my mom keeps that as a memento of my childhood or something.) We chose the smallest bedroom for our office because it looks out onto the rose garden. Jeremy requires a desk and a view when he writes. All I need is my laptop, and I'm good.

We have three romance novels published now, including the one Jeremy wrote alone as Penny James. Those are all selling well, and we have another ready to go. I came into this relationship with about forty bucks in the bank and a mayonnaise jar full of change, but Jeremy had a lot saved from when he practiced law. Add that to the equity he got from selling his Notting Hill place, plus our royalties and the fees we earn from occasional speaking engagements or freelance articles under our author pen name, and we're doing okay financially.

Definitely well enough to afford an apartment. But I'll be good and not mention that today.

We've been working for a while when Jeremy swivels his chair toward the bed where I'm sitting. "What did you think of the cover?"

"Oh. It's finished?"

"He sent it to us last night."

There's a reproof in that comment. One of my jobs is to keep up with our business email, but I forgot to check it before I opened Instagram and sort of lost track of the time.

"Sorry, I'll look at it now." The cover for our next book looks great to me, but Jeremy's picky. "I love it. Why don't you?"

"You don't think it focuses too much on his muscles?"

Silly man. "Eighty-four percent of our readers are women who will swoon over the guy, and the other sixteen percent will picture themselves as him."

He frowns but a few seconds later says, "Approve it then." He swivels back and starts typing.

Okay, time to get to work. I approve the cover. When the designer sends us the final files for print and digital, I can upload them with the interior files. It doesn't seem to be a big deal to Jeremy, so he always lets me have the thrill of clicking those publish buttons. I've been the female half of Penny James for six months, and it's the best job in the world. But even though, with each new book, Jeremy's increased the number of scenes he leaves for me to write, I still can't think of myself as a writer. I mean, I'm writing, yeah, but he's the novelist.

"Word count?"

That's Jeremy-speak for: Are you writing or wasting time?

"How do you expect me to write when you haven't given me the lead-in scene?"

"Working on it."

"You've been saying that for days as you sit there typing away. What are you doing? Starting over every morning?"

"You're a natural at writing romance; I'm not. Just write one of your swoon-worthy sex scenes, and we'll fit it in. Get to it."

"And how can you expect me to write about rapturous love with you nagging me?"

He just smiles.

For a minute, I watch his fingers flying over the keyboard. Such long fingers. Such long, nimble fingers. Fingers that know just where to—okay, I'm inspired now.

Sometime later, I come up for air. Jeremy is still in his chair, but he's watching me.

"Good scene?"

"Very."

"Join me at the club?"

Sometimes, I worry that Jeremy will wake up one day and decide he gave up too much for me. He's had trouble learning to live within our budget. We still took all the California trips we'd planned to research setting locales for our romance series, but we cut costs by staying in motels or B&Bs and eating cheap. That's no big deal to me, but it took a while before Jeremy stopped apologizing that he couldn't pay for the luxury hotels and five-star restaurants he was obviously used to. Going cheaply was no loss to me; I was just thrilled to go.

One of the expenses Jeremy refused to give up was his club membership. I knew from my surveillance last year, when he lived in the apartment above mine, that he went somewhere every afternoon, and then I found out it was his club. I thought he meant an ordinary fitness place. But no. He has a membership in the most exclusive country club in town.

Jeremy pointed out that he'd already paid the one-time—and "much dearer"—initiation costs. (When I asked him how "dear," he told me I didn't want to know.) And surprisingly, though it's considerable on our current budget, the monthly fee is not out of this world, so I agreed not to waste the sign-up costs by canceling unless we absolutely have to. He uses the facilities almost daily, and really, I'm not complaining about the yummy shape it keeps him in.

Right now, I'm sweating on the treadmill next to Jeremy's. "Do you have to run twice as fast and twice as far as me," I ask him.

"I have longer legs than you."

It takes me a second to realize that makes no sense, and when I look at him, he winks. "Ha. Ha."

"Step up your game, Cole, or you'll never make the team."

He's not even breathing hard. I'm just about to call it quits when Scarlett Johansson walks in. She takes the treadmill on Jeremy's other side. Of course she does. Before she even starts to warm up, she sets her treadmill at an incline. Looks like she would have no trouble making his team. And doing it in designer style. Now I feel even more conspicuous than usual in my Target workout clothes.

"I saw they posted the schedule for the tennis tournament," she says to Jeremy. "Are you going to enter?"

"Not this time," he says.

What the hell? He knows her? They've talked before? And he kept that secret from me? This won't do at all.

Think, Chelsea, think.

"Ow." I hit the power button and then nearly fall hopping off the treadmill on one leg.

Jeremy whips his head in my direction. "What happened?"

"Oh, honey, I must have stepped down wrong and twisted something." I'm examining my right foot as if it really hurts.

He steps off his treadmill.

"You should get an icepack on it right away," Scarlett says.

I don't move.

"They have them in the locker room," she adds.

Yeah, like I'm going to leave Jeremy alone with her—well, not alone exactly. At least five other people are in the room. Still.

Jeremy wraps his arm around my waist "Yes, darling, let's go see about that ice."

He helps me limp out of the room but pulls me to a stop in the hallway. "You are so obvious," he says, but he's grinning.

"Why didn't you tell me you're friends with frigging Scarlett Johansson?"

His brows rise. "Friends? I played tennis with her husband once."

"Oh."

"Ohhh." He taps the tip of my nose. "I'm certain your foot is magically healed now, so shall we change for the pool? I'll have to swim twice as many laps to make up for the short run."

Every time I say I'll come to the club with him, he asks if I'd like to play tennis, which is my fault because I sort of told him I knew how, but I don't. I mean I know the rules. I just suck at actually playing, but maybe I should at least watch if he's going to be playing with gorgeous celebrities.

I swim with him for a while. Well, not actually with him because he's in the lap pool, but it's right next to this one. At least swimming is something I excel at—I mean, not competitively or anything, like Jeremy did in school, but I've known how to swim since I was a baby. But I've done it mostly in the ocean while surfing, so by comparison, the pool is a bore. After twenty minutes or so, I'm done. I swim to the edge and look for Scarlett because if she's here, I'll have to limp when I get out of the pool. Oh. My. God. Is that Matthew McConaughey walking toward the parking lot? Dang. I really should come here more often.

I slip on my sunglasses and settle down to lounge by the pool while Jeremy finishes his workout. He also plays golf here, but I told the truth about not playing that. Then he found out my mom does, so now they're both bugging me to learn. Jeremy points out the driving range every time we come here. I swear the next time he brings it up, I'm going to make a deal with him—I'll learn to play golf if he learns to surf. With his weird aversion to sand, that should end the discussion. Oh, wait. Maybe I should ask who he plays golf with.

As it often does when I'm not distracted, my thoughts turn to writing. Romantic suspense, huh? I had another idea in mind: sports-themed romances. With my surfing knowledge, and Jeremy's sports experience, I thought we could come up with several ideas for a series. I've already had fun outlining the first two novels. But it's Jeremy's call. Still … maybe I'll show him my ideas.

My eyes fly open when cold drops hit my stomach. Jeremy's standing over me dripping water.

"You ready to leave?" he says. "Or would you like to try out the driving range first?"

I run my nails down his thigh. "I'd rather go home and play in our bed."

He grins and pulls me to my feet.

I know. I know. But hey, when I'm this close to a handsome, nearly naked man, can you blame me?

Jeremy has the most gorgeous eyes, sometimes blue, sometimes green, and always sexy … well, except when he's angry, but that's not often. Right now, his eyes are heating up my girly parts. I swear, just that look gets me halfway to orgasm. (No wonder women gobble up his romances.)

He lies down beside me, propping his head on one hand, and traces a finger from my bottom lip to my navel. Slowly. Oh, so deliciously slow. When he leans closer to kiss me, his hair falls forward, a dark curtain, hiding our faces.

"You were the most beautiful woman at the pool."

I wasn't.

"All the men were looking at you."

They weren't.

"Do you know how happy I am that you're all mine?"

"Will you show me?"

"Oh, yes." He kisses my throat.

"Yes." He licks my nipples.

"Yes." He slips fingers inside me. Those long, nimble fingers.

Oh, yes. Yes. Yes.

For a moment, he's hot and hard against my thigh, and then he slides down, pulling me to the foot of the bed, pulling me to him. Kneeling on the floor, he slips his hands under my ass and lifts slightly, bringing me to his mouth as if I'm a delicious pastry he means to devour. And he does.

For hours, it seems, we are lost in a place both inside and out, filled with moans and cries and husky-voiced whispers. And finally, when he withdraws from me, leaving a bit of himself behind, his hot, herbal life essence, a kind of treasure just for me, I'm thankful that monogamy makes condoms no longer necessary.

"I love you," I say for the thousandth time.

"You are my life." His voice is already thick with impending sleep.

Jeremy has the most perfect profile. Actually, he has the most perfect face at any angle, but I love lying beside him and watching him sleep. I want to talk to him now, though, so I slide my finger down the slope of his nose. He always wakes with a jerk and looks around as though he can never remember where he fell asleep. I think that's funny, but if he ever looks over at me and seems surprised, the dude's in trouble.

"Hello, gorgeous," he says.

"Hello, handsome. I need your help with something."

He grins. "Good God, you're insatiable."

I smack his chest. "Not that. I want your input on the wedding."

"Right. Well … I'm all for it."

Ten seconds later, he's halfway to sleep again.

"Jeremy."

His eyes fly open. He turns on his side toward me, his serious face in place. "Ask away."

"You've never told me what kind of wedding you imagined you'd have."

He taps the tip of my nose. "I can't say I ever gave it any thought."

"None?"

"To be honest …" He presses his lips together and looks away for a second. "I guess I assumed my betrothed would make all the decisions and just tell me when and where to show up."

"So if I want to invite five hundred guests, you're okay with that?"

His eyes widen. "Do you?"

"No. What if I want to marry at midnight with everyone wearing black."

"I'll tell your mother."

"Be serious."

"I am serious about that."

"You're not any help." I get up and start getting dressed.

He sits up. "As long as it's you standing before me saying, 'I do,' that's all I care about. Truly."

"Check and check. What kind of wedding will your family expect?"

His eyes narrow. "My sister and uncle won't care a whit. They'll just be happy for us."

He knows I'm inviting his parents and brother, so why does he pretend I'm not? But I'm sure any wedding we can afford won't impress them. Not a "whit."

"And I thought you'd left all this planning up to Gabi."

Sigh. "I have to give her some direction. What do you want to wear—and if you say clothes, I'll give you another black eye."

"I've always suspected that wasn't an accident," he says. "You and your kinky ways of drawing me into your lair."

"Ha. Ha." He knows damn well that was accidental. He'd paid me to read his first book, and I was anxious to give him my feedback. So when I heard him leave his apartment, I rushed to catch him coming down the stairs, but when I jerked open the door, he was standing there, getting ready to knock, and it startled me, so I punched him automatically out of self-defense. That could happen to anyone. "So, what's your answer?"

"Well, I was thinking a nude wedding would be quite nice, but I expect that's out of the question."

"Ha. Ha."

"Right. So it's still a beach wedding?"

"Yes."

"Casual, then."

"No, they set it up like a regular wedding, with an aisle and a gazebo or something where we'll stand for the ceremony."

"Formal?"

"Yes."

He reaches for his underwear. "To avoid any misunderstanding, explain what formal means to you."

"I'll be wearing a full-length, white monstrosity of a wedding dress."

"Right." He stands to zip his jeans. "So ... morning coat?"

Yeah, like I know what that is. I'm sorry I started this conversation. "Never mind. The rental place will help you pick out something."

"Rental place?"

"You want to buy a tux ... or whatever?"

His eyes slide away for a second. Way to go, Chelsea, you've reminded him he's not rich anymore. "I mean ... we could look for a deal. They must have sales on men's formal wear too, right?"

"Actually, I don't need to buy. Or rent."

"Oh." He owns a tux and, evidently, this morning coat thing? I glance at the closet.

"Some of my clothes are in our storage facility," he says.

"I thought that was just your heaviest winter stuff."

He shrugs. "That too."

"Okay, so I guess you're prepared for any eventuality."

He cocks a brow. "Are you mocking me?"

"No, I think that's great. It will save us money."

He narrows his eyes and studies me for a moment. "Did you not hear what you said?"

I think back, but I don't come up with anything that would confuse or anger him. I shake my head.

"Since when do you say things like for any eventuality?" Grinning, he takes me in his arms. "You're adorable."

I'm not stupid enough to argue.

three

Jeremy's sitting at his desk this morning, and I'm across the room on the twin bed where I'm supposed to be reading the scene he finally produced, but I'm watching him instead. His face is turned toward the window, but I get the sense he's not really seeing what's outside. He's not working. When he's working out some story thing in his head, his fingers move slightly like he's typing. Right now, his hands are still. What does he think about when he drifts away like this?

"Jeremy? Who's this uncle you want to invite to the wedding?"

He swivels his chair toward me. "Uncle Bert … Albert. My father's brother."

"He's your favorite uncle?"

"My only uncle. But he'd be my favorite even if I had ten uncles. I used to wish he was my father."

Does he not know the tone in his voice says he still wishes that? "Tell me about him."

"He's … jolly. He finds something to laugh about in almost any situation. He's kindhearted and quite intelligent."

I think I already know the answer, but I'll ask anyway. "How did he feel about you quitting law?"

"He told me life's too short not to follow your heart."

Look at the way talking about his uncle makes him smile. "Sounds like opposite brothers run in your family."

"Apparently."

"I can't wait to meet Uncle Bert. I love him already."

"He'll love you too."

"So why don't you take me to meet him in England?"

Wow! That smile vanished fast.

"How many times are we going to have that conversation?"

Until you give in. "Tell me more about your uncle. Is he married?"

His glare takes a few seconds to melt away. "He was. A long time ago. She died when I was four, I think. I barely remember her."

"And he never remarried?"

"No. He travels a lot. Lives in a small flat when he's in London. He used to live with us in the country house, but he moved out and into a cottage on the grounds after Aunt Lou died."

"The country house?"

"Hmm? Oh. The family home. Where I grew up."

"I thought your parents lived in the city."

"Well … yes, they have a place there too. Because … my father works in the city. And my mother … has friends and … things she does there."

"Uh-huh." How should I decipher that response? "I know so little about you, Jeremy. You won't even tell me about you as a boy."

"That's not true. I've told you many stories."

"Mostly about you and Ethan as high school … I mean secondary school and college roommates. What about your childhood?"

"I've told you stories about my sister and me."

"Three incidents. Maybe. I hardly know anything about what you were like as a boy. Without Ethan. Without Laura. Not even what you looked like."

"Yes, you do. Laura texted you a photo."

One. And he was eighteen. My mom has photos of me all over the house, and he's studied them all—including that horrible seventh-grade school photo, taken the day after Gabi and I dyed my hair black with blonde chunks—not highlights, chunks. And the photo albums. Oh. My. God. He's seen every photo of me that was ever taken and he thinks I should be satisfied with one photo of him. No way, dude. I'll see them all when we go to London, which I'm now determined to do if I have to knock him out and ship him there in a dog cage.

"One little photo from your sister doesn't tell me much."

"Tell Laura to bring more when she comes over in May."

He's being deliberately dense, so I give up. For now. "What were you thinking while you were looking out the window?"

He turns back to his desk. "What to write for the next scene."

"No, you weren't."

He faces the window again and doesn't answer for a moment. "It's my mum's birthday."

His mum? He's never called her that to me before … and I doubt he's aware he did now. A quick look at the world clock on my phone tells me it's already 7:12 p.m. in London. "Have you talked to her today?"

He shakes his head.

I walk over to his desk and pick up his phone. "Call her."

He just looks at me.

"Call her now."

He takes the phone from me, so I leave the room to give him privacy. But I don't close the door all the way until I hear him speak.

I'm sort of shocked that Jeremy told me he'd been thinking about his mother. Getting him to open up about his parents is almost impossible. I know at least one of them phones him once a week, or more, but he always leaves the room to talk to them. And he usually needs cheering up afterward, which is why I'm baking him cookies now. Chocolate chips with pecans are his favorite, so my mom keeps the ingredients on hand at all times, and since she's not here, we can pig out on cookies for lunch if we want to.

He walks into the kitchen just as I slide the first batch in the oven. His face doesn't reflect the impact of the conversation he had with his mother. Surely, she was in a good mood on her birthday. Then again, at her age—which I don't know but assume it's close to my mom's—she might have been depressed about getting older. Not that my mom gets depressed on her birthdays. She's always happy just to be alive.

"Cookies for lunch," I tell him.

He pulls me into his arms and holds me tight. Does this mean the conversation with his mother sucked? I lay my head against his chest and listen to his heartbeat, pounding at first. He doesn't loosen his grip on me until it slows.

"Chocolate chip?" he says.

"Of course. All you can eat."

"Have I told you I love you?"

"Once or twice."

He takes his phone from his pocket and types something. A few seconds later, my text message alert sounds.

I love you. I love you. I love you. I love you. I love you. I love you. I love you.

We're still kissing when the oven timer buzzes. I take the cookies from the oven and start moving them, one by one, to the cooling rack. Sometimes, like now, when Jeremy texts me, I flash back to the horrible mess last September when his phone was stolen on his way to London, and we lost communication for a couple of days. I thought he'd left me, so when he got a new phone and started calling and texting, I ignored him. Worst week of my life. But followed by a wonderful week of make-up sex.

"You're thinking about sex, aren't you?" he says.

"Mind reading?"

"No, you were smiling to yourself. That particular smile."

"I have a sex smile?"

"You do. Wait. Don't put that pan in the oven yet."

"Why?"

"I believe it's my duty to do something about that smile."

I set down the cookie sheet. "Do you?"

"Yes. But I'm not sure what."

I grab him by his shirt and pull him toward our room. "Let me educate you, sir."

"Hot damn."

Cookies and sex—two ways to a man's heart.

♥ ♥ ♥

Unlike Gabi, when I was growing up, I didn't think a lot about marriage and motherhood and all that jazz. I mean, I thought a lot about dreamy guys and what having sex would be like, but my daydreams kind of faded to black after that point. And even though I always figured I'd get married, now that I'm actually going to do it, I'm prone to panic any time of day or night. One time, the seriousness of it hit me so hard I stopped dead in the middle of the frozen food aisle at Von's and caused the woman behind me to rear-end me with her cart.

I'm going to be a wife in four months.

A wife.

Four months.

Sometimes, when I think about that, I can't breathe. Like right now.

It's not that I'm afraid getting married is a mistake. And certainly not that it's a mistake to marry Jeremy. He'll be a great husband—seriously, how could he not be? But what if I screw it up? I don't buy into that if it doesn't work, get a divorce mind-set. So I have to make my marriage work. And I'd have a lot more confidence that I could if we were living on our own now. Why doesn't Jeremy understand that?

I save the scene I'm working on and close my laptop. "I want to move."

Jeremy sighs but doesn't turn from his desk. "We've talked about this a thousand times."

"Okay. Let's talk about it a thousand and one times."

"I'm in the middle of something."

"Well, now you're already out of the zone, so we might as well talk."

Total, complete, utter silence. It's like I never spoke. So that's it. End of discussion.

I text Gabi.

> **Talk to me.**
> **What's up?**

What if I'm a terrible wife?

As the first notes of "Baby One More Time" play, Gabi's face pops up on my screen. (What can I say? Britney Spears was hot when Gabi and I became friends.) I tap to answer.

"Hey, Gabs." I have no intention of discussing my marriage fears in front of Jeremy, so before he can give me the not-while-I'm-working glare, I leave the room.

"Get a grip, Chels. There's no way you'll mess this up. There's no way Jeremy will let you. He's so in love with you, I think he'd overlook anything you do rather than lose you. Hell, he might even agree to let you have a lover on the side."

"Ha. Ha. He won't even agree to take me to London to meet his parents."

"Maybe he's afraid they'll turn you against him."

"As if."

"True." Ice clinking against glass fills my ear, and then she continues. "It'll suck if you have to meet them for the first time at your wedding."

"That's what I told him."

"And what did he say?"

"He told me not to invite them."

"Like that's going to stop you."

I smile. "Yeah, I'll get their address from Laura."

More ice clinking.

"Does she have an explanation why Jeremy's so stubborn about his parents?" she asks.

"It's weird, but when I ask her, she sounds like she's hiding something. I think Jeremy's told her not to talk to me about them."

Gabi laughs. "Is he blackmailing her or something?"

"Who knows?"

"I think it's weird they haven't even acknowledged your

engagement," she says. "I would never have married Matt without meeting his family first."

"Matt's family lives only three hours away."

"And Jeremy's family is rich. They could fly here to meet you. And even if, for some reason, they couldn't do that, there's always Skype."

"You're forgetting that Matt's parents love him and you."

"True." She sighs. "I just can't believe Jeremy's parents are so cold toward him. He's a great guy."

"Thanks. But apparently, with them, you do what you're told, or you're blacklisted. I don't know if they'll ever forgive him for giving up a law career."

"So you're just going to avoid the Pearces forever?"

"I don't want to. I'm not exactly anxious to meet them, but still. My mom's been hinting that maybe she should make the first move."

"Well, if you won't—"

"I can't."

"Yeah, Chels, because we both know how shy you are."

"I mean, I can't let my mom contact his parents because they … don't know."

"Don't know what?"

Sigh. "That I exist."

Gabi's silence is because she's waiting for me to laugh. When I don't, she gasps.

"Seriously? And why don't they know you exist?"

"Jeremy never told them." I picture her eyes nearly popping out of her head.

"That's fucked up, Chelsea. What the hell? He's just been using you? I'll kill him."

"No. You've got it wrong." I take a deep breath. "He didn't really want to tell them, and … I was okay with that."

"Why the hell am I just finding out about this? Never mind. Whatever you were going to say won't make a bit of sense to me."

"It doesn't make sense to me either—now. We can't just surprise them with a wedding invitation. We have to tell them."

"No shit." She sighs. "So why didn't Jeremy want them to know you're engaged?"

"I guess he thought they'd give him more grief about not marrying Alison."

"You guess? Jesus, Chelsea, maybe you guys should have a real conversation once in a while."

"Yeah. Hey, I gotta go, but we'll see you tomorrow."

I pocket my phone and creep back into the office so I don't disturb Jeremy again. Maybe I'll write a scene where the hero refuses to invite his parents to his wedding because he's a stubborn ass. See what he says about that.

♥ ♥ ♥

Matt and Jeremy have become close friends, which is great for Gabi and me. It's Super Bowl day, so we're at Sunset Brewhouse, where even Jeremy can find a beer that meets his standards. The guys are watching the game on the TV across from our table, but Gabi and I are looking through an issue of *Brides*.

"What do you think of this dress?" she asks.

"It's beautiful, but kind of … traditional."

"A wedding is a traditional occasion, Chels. Were you planning to just hot glue some lace onto one of your tank top and shorts ensembles? Don't forget to glue crystals on your flip-flops too."

"Ooh, pregnancy is making you quite the bitch."

She smiles and pats her stomach. "Nine more weeks."

Her baby bump is the cutest thing. It really does look like she stuffed a volleyball under her shirt.

"I can't wait for this baby to get here."

"And you're also terrified."

"Damn straight." She looks wistfully at my margarita. "And I can't even have a drink to chill."

We both jump when the guys react loudly to something in the game. A love of sports is one thing they share. Matt's recruited Jeremy to join his softball team for the summer. I can't believe it's been only seven months since Gabi secretly arranged my first date with Jeremy after one of Matt's games.

"Earth to Chelsea." Gabi's pointing to another dress in the magazine.

"Nah. I don't like that one either. Sorry. I wouldn't feel like myself."

Gabi holds up the magazine to show Jeremy. "What do you think of this dress?" No response. "Jeremy."

He tears his eyes away from the game long enough to look at the photo. "You've chosen that dress?"

"No, we're asking your opinion of it."

His eyes are already back on the game. "Nice, but that's not Chelsea."

"Told you."

She sighs and puts the magazine away. "So, do you think his parents will come to the wedding?"

The place is so loud now, Jeremy probably didn't hear her question, but I glance at him to check. He's totally concentrating on the TV. I scoot closer to Gabi so we can talk quieter and still hear each other. "They're getting an invitation, but who knows if they'll accept. I'm still trying to convince him I need to meet them before then."

"I know they don't approve of his new career, but it seems awfully drastic to reject him over that. And it certainly won't help things if they get a wedding invitation out of the blue."

"Exactly. Tell Matt to work on him. Maybe he can change his mind."

She shakes her head. "There's probably some man code against that. We don't want to risk their friendship." She grins. "You know what I heard Matt say the other day when he smashed his thumb trying to put the crib together? He yelled bloody hell, just like Jeremy does."

"And Jeremy sounds more American since they've been hanging out."

"Ow." Gabi presses on the lump visible through the fabric stretched tightly across her baby bump. "With all this punting, I don't have any doubt B.G. will be athletic.

(B.G. stands for boy or girl, which is what we call the baby because Gabi and Matt opted to wait for the birth to learn the sex.)

Gabi takes a sip of her iced tea. "Have you and Jeremy talked about having kids yet?"

"I'm just not sure I'm mother material, so I haven't brought it up. And neither has he." She gives me that look. "We'll talk about it. The wedding's not until May."

"It's already February."

Suddenly the noise level in the place rockets and so do most of the people, including Jeremy and Matt. I glance up at the TV just as the fourth quarter ends. By the gleeful high-fives and backslapping our guys are giving, I assume their team won. Matt motions for our server to bring another round.

"Not for me," I call to her. "We can't both get drunk," I

say in answer to Jeremy's questioning look. "Gabi's driving them home. Who did you think was driving us, Mr. I-Don't-Want-to-Uber?"

He gives me a thumbs-up. "You two have the wedding plans sorted now, eh?"

Gabi sighs as I roll my eyes. Men are so naive about these things.

"We've just begun," she says.

Jeremy looks astonished at that news. "But … you talk about it every day."

Matt elbows him. "It's shopping, man.

"Ah, right." Jeremy nods, "And women can't make up their minds what to buy until they've tried on every damned thing in the mall."

They grin and fist-bump.

"Ha. Ha." Gabi and I chorus.

"You guys going to have kids right away?" Matt asks.

Jeremy doesn't miss a beat. "I'm definitely in favor of pro-creating, but maybe we should wait a while to see how it goes for you two."

The server sets down their beers and Gabi's iced tea. I grab the tea and take a long drink, hoping they'll forget I didn't respond to the question. But when I set it down, Matt and Jeremy are still looking at me, so I have to say something.

"Yeah. I feel exactly the same way."

Gabi whips her head in my direction, but I don't look at her.

four

A couple of days later, I'm at Gabi's to help her finish decorating the nursery, which means I'm mostly holding things up against the wall while she stands back to see where they look best. The room looks so sweet and peaceful. I'm a little bit envious—even though picturing myself as a mother freaks me out. But Jeremy wants to be a father. I just can't think about that now.

When we finish with the nursery, Gabi pulls me into the dining room to her laptop. After she shows me the photos of the wedding venue, she hands me the printout of her wedding plan spreadsheet. As I scan the cost estimates, my excitement sinks until it's draining right out my toes. There's no way we can afford all this, and even if my mom could, I wouldn't let her pay this much. Gabi, as usual, reads my mind.

"It's a once in a lifetime experience, Chels … at least, it's supposed to be."

"I know." I hand back the spreadsheet. "And I appreciate how hard you've worked on this, but I can't do it. I can't afford this. We aren't going into debt for the next fifty years over our wedding." I'm breaking her heart. "I'm sorry, Gabi."

"It wasn't that much work, silly."

"I mean, I know this is what you wanted."

"What?"

I point to the gorgeous wedding scene displayed on her laptop. "That's what you dreamed of having."

"Well, yeah. Not at the beach, but—"

"Just as beautiful."

"What does that have to do with your wedding?"

"You didn't get to—"

"Ohmygod, you thought I wanted to help you so I could pretend I was planning my wedding?" She smacks my arm and then grabs me in a hug. "You idiot." She releases me and then smacks me again. "It's your day, Chels. What do you want?"

"I don't know."

"Of course you do."

I try to picture Jeremy and me saying our vows. Vows. Oh God. By summer, I'll be Mrs. Jeremy Windsor Pearce ... well, unless I decide to keep my last name, but I probably won't ... or I could hyphenate ... or just have two last names.

"Chelsea?"

"Huh? Oh, yeah." I point to the photo on her laptop. "That's too elaborate. Too big."

"Okay, a simple, intimate wedding. Check. What else? Still the beach?"

"Well ..." I pause when Gabi bites her lower lip. I'm being difficult. "I don't think Jeremy's too crazy about a beach wedding."

"Yeah, I know. He thinks it will be too windy. And sandy."

"And just how do you know that?"

"He told Matt, and Matt told me, even though he wasn't supposed to, and now I'm telling you, even though I promised not to." She rolls her eyes, and we both laugh. Then she shoots me a dead serious look. "You and Jeremy still need to work on your communication skills."

I can't argue with that. Well, it's really just Jeremy that sucks at communication. He keeps too much to himself and sometimes just assumes I know what he's thinking, but I don't because he keeps too much to himself. His lack of communication nearly kept us from getting engaged in the first place. He ran off to London with his previous fiancée—well, she wasn't really his fiancée, and he didn't actually go to London with her, but I thought he did, so I almost started a relationship with my old surfing idol, Dusty Haines.

"Earth to Chelsea."

"Huh? Oh. So Jeremy's just going along with what I want instead of telling me the truth about what he wants? Geez. I'm not a crazy person that everyone has to placate to keep from flipping out."

"No, you're just someone who lies to her fiancé about how she feels about having children."

"I didn't lie. I just realized that what Jeremy said was sensible, so I agreed."

"Because you always go for sensible, right?" She waits a beat before she smiles to take the edge off that barb. "Come on. I told Luisa I'd bring you to Mama Mia's today."

I've been avoiding Mama Mia's because the owner, Luisa, is like a grandmother to me, so she knows all about the wedding, and I'm sure she's waiting for me to ask her to cater it or at least book the rehearsal dinner, probably both. But though her food is fantastic, I think we should go a little more upscale. I'm assuming Jeremy's parents will attend the wedding dinner, at least, and I can't picture them being comfortable with her homestyle Italian food. (Yes, I hate myself a little for that.)

When we enter, I brace myself for Luisa's usual enthusiastic greeting, which is both tactile and deafening.

"Ah, my beautiful Chelsea!" As usual, Luisa directs her hug to my face, not my body, squishing my cheeks like they're bread dough. But today it's short-lived because she has to greet Gabi too.

"And my beautiful Gabriella." As she kneads Gabi's cheeks, Luisa rattles off some Italian, which Gabi understands because her mother taught her the language so she could communicate with her grandparents. "Go. Sit. Sit. I bring you soup that will make you cry with love."

"Don't mention the wedding," I say when we find a table. Gabi gives me a look and shakes her head. She disapproves of my worrying about what Jeremy's parents will think of me.

One of Luisa's granddaughters serves our soup, but Luisa's right behind her. "When you finish your soup," she says, "I bring you a little pasta, but not too much. You must have room for dessert … something special today." She screws her finger into her cheek. "Delizioso!"

"I heard about this new bridal shop," Gabi says when Luisa leaves us alone. "Why don't we go check it out after lunch?"

"Maybe."

"Chelsea, you haven't liked any dress you've tried on so far, and if you're going to special order one, we're running out of time."

"I know." I concentrate on my soup, which really is delicious, but if I cry today, I'm pretty sure it won't be over this taste. "Do you know what a morning coat is?"

"They've been pictured in every wedding magazine I've shown you."

"Right. Well, Jeremy owns one … and a tux." Gabi's eyes widen. "Now do you see why I'm worried about fitting in with his family?"

She takes a sip of water. "Yeah, I get it. But from what he says, Jeremy doesn't fit in either, so why should you?"

"You're disgustingly positive since you got pregnant, you know that?"

We make it through the pasta and two unnecessary appearances of Luisa at our table, without any mention of the wedding. Then she brings out a small cake, one that looks suspiciously like a miniature wedding cake.

"My daughter, Mirella, you remember her, Chelsea? She moves here now and opens a bakery." Luisa cuts two slices and puts one in front of me and the other in front of Gabi. "Eat. Eat. This will break your heart it's so delicious."

Gabi and I each take a bite. It's heaven in my mouth, and the look Gabi gives me says she thinks so too.

"Everything my Mirella bake"—Luisa kisses her fingertips—"è perfetto."

"Does she make wedding cakes?" Gabi asks.

Luisa smiles and pulls a business card from her apron pocket.

All but assured her daughter will bake my cake and no doubt hoping she'll be providing the wedding food, Luisa wouldn't let us pay for our lunch.

"The bridal shop is only ten minutes from here," Gabi says on the way out.

Sigh. "All right."

Gabi looks at me over the roof of the car. "Answer me honestly, Chels. Are you having second thoughts about marrying Jeremy?"

"Seriously? No, no, no, a million times, no! Let's go. Another shop full of ridiculous wastes of money awaits."

The shop is named Le Jour, which even my mono-language brain can translate.

"Just don't pick an ugly dress for your matron of honor," Gabi says as she turns off the engine.

"Wouldn't dream of it." We both know she'll be choosing hers and the bridesmaids' dresses. Who am I kidding? She'll choose my dress too. Fashion is her expertise, not mine.

A classy electronic tone sounds when I open the door. We step inside, instantly engulfed by so much fluffy whiteness, it's like we're standing inside a wedding cake. A pale, pale woman dressed in pale, pale gray seems to float toward us through this whipped cream nightmare. Even her hair is white, though her glasses are severe in shape and black rimmed. She's scowling at my hair. Purple underlayers are probably an abomination in this place.

The salesclerk addresses Gabi. "Good afternoon. May I help you?"

"I'm looking for a wedding dress," I say.

"Of course," she says, her voice dripping with disappointment that I'm the one who'll be trying on her precious gowns. "When is the wedding?"

"In May."

I translate her raised brows.

"Well, let's hope we have something in stock." She looks me up and down. "Will you be losing any weight before the wedding?"

What the hell? "I'm a size six."

"Yes." The tone in her voice insinuates I doubt that or else size six is enormous.

"Ivory or white?"

I'm so tempted to say black, but a warning look from Gabi keeps my mouth shut.

"Why don't you show us some of both?" she says to Ms. Frosty.

So begins two hours of trying on one hideous dress after another. All of them wrong for me. This one has too many layers. That one makes me look like a fairy. Another poufs in all the wrong places, while the next squeezes my hips and swallows my breasts. And forget the ones with yards of fabric swirled at my feet. With me wearing it, that's an accident waiting to happen. Satin, organza, silk, crepe, chiffon, and let's not forget the ever-exotic charmeuse. And all of them with too many pearls or crystals or nameless sparkly bits. Hand sewn—but of course!

"Perhaps it's the hair," Ms. Frosty says, clearly exasperated. "Most brides like to see themselves in the dress with their hair styled and colored as they'll be wearing it on their wedding day."

"Oh, right, I guess I should have added the turquoise streaks before I came here."

I swear the woman turns to a pillar of ice. Standing behind her, Gabi tries to shoot me a deadly look, but she's fighting not to grin.

"That was a joke," I say.

Ms. Frozen's lips twitch in what I presume passes for a smile. "We might receive a few more styles on Tuesday."

"Thank you," Gabi says. "We'll be back."

Like hell we will. As far as I'm concerned, I won't be anywhere in this vicinity on Tuesday or any other day.

"Lovely," drones the human iceberg. With a flick of her hand, she dismisses me to put on my own clothes and get the hell out of her domain.

"Sorry we never got to look for your dress," I tell Gabi as the shop door closes behind us.

"Your dress is the important one. But come on, Chels. You don't seem to have any style in mind."

"I'm not trying to be difficult. Seriously, did you think any of those suited me?"

She doesn't answer until we're back in the car. "Not really. Some of them were beautiful, but ..."

"Yeah, but. Maybe Jeremy's right; we should have a nude wedding."

She casts a sideways withering glare at me. "I'd kill you first."

♥ ♥ ♥

My mom's been acting weird all day, distracted and jumpy, so even though I cooked dinner, I volunteer me and Jeremy to do the cleaning up. When he's done loading the dishwasher, he rubs a hand across his midriff. He loves my mom's cooking but worries he'll gain weight. Right now, I'll bet he's planning a more rigorous workout for tomorrow. Fine with me. If he starts letting himself go now, what will he look like ten years after we're married? I try to picture him with a beer belly and receding hairline. Nope. My brain won't go there. My mom looks great for her age, and it's not like she exercises much, so I hope I've inherited those genes. But to be safe, maybe I should work out tomorrow too.

I used to keep in shape by going to the beach as often as I could, but I never surf and don't even get much use out of my boogie board since I met Jeremy. He doesn't mind if I go with my old friends once in a while, but I feel guilty leaving him. Plus, I know the reason he quizzes me on who I'll be with is because my beach days always remind him of Dusty, the surfing champ he thinks he almost lost me to. As if.

Jeremy smacks my ass as we're about to leave the kitchen. "Want to join me at the club tomorrow?"

"Is that your way of telling me I'm getting fat?"

He winks at me. "You have only the perfect amount of fat in all the right places, which are the places I was thinking about when I slapped your bum."

"Oh, that. Reason number one thous—"

"Yes, yes, I know."

"Remember the night we got engaged … on the beach?"

"Yes, I remember, and that's why I'll wait until we can do it in our totally sand-free bed, thank you very much."

It's cute that Jeremy says "totally" and "seriously" like me now. Not that I want him to lose his accent, but I'm glad he's adopted some SoCal-speak, which he still sometimes mocks as "California Girlese," because now when he's in one of his talkative moods, I don't have to translate in my head as much as I used to. It's cut down on my misunderstanding him —"getting the short end of the stick" as Jeremy says.

We join my mother in the living room for an episode of Game of Thrones—or two; I think we're behind. She doesn't enjoy it as much as we do, but she'll do anything for Jeremy.

Just as we walk in, my mom's phone rings, and she jumps a mile. She glances at Jeremy before she looks at her phone screen. "It's Marianne," she says and leaves the room.

"Did my mom sound ridiculously relieved to you?"

"When?"

"Just now, when she said it was her friend calling."

"I didn't notice." Jeremy turns on the TV and brings up HBO On Demand. "You think she was lying? Could it have been a man calling?"

"I doubt it."

"Doesn't your mother date?" He scrolls through to the episode we'll watch first but doesn't start it. "She hasn't since we've been living here, at least not that I know, but surely she does."

"Would you be jealous?"

His face warps in horror. "What a preposterous question."

So quickly he reverts to Mr. High Tea-speak.

"Chill, dude." I curl up next to him on the sofa. "She dates, just not often. I think she still misses my dad too much."

"That's why she's so close to you. And why we're living here."

"We're living here because you said we couldn't afford—"

He shakes his head. "That was for her benefit. She's not ready to let you go."

"You're crazy. I was living away from her for over a year."

"But for most of that time you were still hers. Now you're mine."

"What am I—a pet?" I scoot away from him.

He pulls me back. "Don't play that feminism card with me. I used to be Penny James, you know."

"Used to be?"

"I'm back," my mom announces.

Jeremy picks up the remote, but I elbow him.

"That was a pretty quick conversation," I say. "Usually you and Marianne talk for an hour."

"Oh … she just had a quick question." She shoots another split-second glance at Jeremy.

Got it. Don't ask in front of Jeremy. I miss a good ten minutes of GoT before I quit trying to figure out that phone call.

At first, it ticked me off that Jeremy falls right to sleep after we have sex, but I quickly learned that he *always* earns his rest. Tonight, I'm glad he's asleep because I want to talk to my mom without him knowing. I slip out of bed and into some pjs. I'm sure my mom's asleep by now, but she won't mind me waking her. We've had some of our best chats at midnight in the glow from her bedside lamp.

I'm surprised to see that light on when I open her door a crack. "Mom?"

"Come in, sweetie." She lays aside her book and takes off her reading glasses.

The familiar sweet scent in the room hits me immediately. All my life, it's smelled of the ylang-ylang candles she burns in here.

"I'm glad you're awake," I say. Though my dad died almost four years ago, she still sleeps on her side of their sleigh bed, so I sit against the footboard on his side, facing her. "What's up with that phone call?"

She looks like I just slapped her. "How did you know?"

"We were in the room when your phone rang."

"Oh, that call." She lays a hand on her chest, obviously relieved. "Marianne."

"But it wasn't really Marianne, was it? You looked at Jeremy—twice. And you've acted weird all day."

She covers her face with her hands. "Oh, Chelsea, I've done something terrible. Well, it wouldn't have been quite so terrible if you and Jeremy hadn't—" She shakes her head. "No, I can't pass the blame. It's fully my—"

"Mom. You're freaking me out. What are you talking about?"

"The caller tonight was Marianne, but I was afraid it was Amanda calling again, though with the time difference, I should have known it wasn't."

"Mom." I think she's lost her mind. "Who's Amanda?"

"Amanda Pearce."

Now, I feel like I'm losing it. "Jeremy's mother? How do you know—ohmygod." I rocket to my feet. "Did his father have a heart attack? Is he dead?"

"Chelsea, calm down. Don't you think I would have told Jeremy immediately if something had happened to his father?"

"I don't know, Mom. None of this is making sense." I sit back down. "Since when does Jeremy's mother call you? And why? And how the hell did she get your cell number?"

My mom's too polite to roll her eyes, but she's doing this eyes-wide-lips-pursed thing that means the same.

"I've talked to her twice. Today. I called her first, this morning." She looks me in the eye, waiting, as though I'm supposed to make something of that.

"Okay. So you called her this morning, and then she called you back. What did you talk—oh. Oh no. Oh fuck."

"Exactly. Evidently, it's no surprise to you that she had no idea who I am—who you are, for that matter. Our conversation was awkward and upsetting for us both."

"You shouldn't have called her, Mom. Jeremy said he'd talk to his parents about the trip. It wasn't your place to—" I stop talking because her eyes are glistening.

"I'm sorry, sweetie. I sincerely wish I hadn't made the call. Jeremy's going to be furious with me, isn't he?"

"No, he won't." Yes, he will. "You're right. We should have told them about our engagement weeks ago. Months ago. So … now they know."

"I'm sorry for interfering."

"It's okay. Really." I fake a smile and crawl to the head of the bed to hug her. "How did his mother react?"

"Well, she sounded a lot calmer than I felt. She asked a lot of questions about you. And then she asked about the wedding plans. I couldn't tell her much about those, of course. She put me on hold for a minute, and when she came back, she asked about our schedules for March. I told her—well, I wasn't sure about yours and Jeremy's, but I said I didn't think there was anything important, so I hope I didn't—"

"Mom."

"Oh. Yes, well, then she asked if she could call me back."

"And she did."

"Yes, about an hour later. She wanted to know if we would be free to visit the first two weeks of March, and by then, I'd asked you what you had coming up in March, so I told—"

"They're coming here?"

"Well … no."

"Oh, wow." I jump off the bed again. "We're going to London."

She pats the bed beside her, and I sit. She takes my hand. "Aren't you forgetting something, sweetie?"

"Oh, yeah. A passport. I forgot to tell you I got one months ago. I didn't even tell Jeremy, but I figured—"

"Chelsea?" She's questioning me with a look.

"What?" She just keeps looking at me. "Oh crap. Jeremy."

"That's why I wanted to talk to you first."

"He's already said he won't go."

"Which I told his mother."

I'm stunned. She always tries hard not to hurt someone's feelings. "I can't believe you told her that."

"I hated to, but she left me no choice. She made it sound like you didn't want to meet them, and I couldn't let her think that."

"What did she say when you told her it was Jeremy who said no?"

"Well, first she sighed—you know, like she'd heard that a hundred times? Then she said, 'Jeremy will come.' And I told her, if she could convince him to, I'd be happy to buy the tickets, but"—she closes her eyes for a second and gives a quick shake of her head—"Amanda said she'd already booked the flight. Isn't that odd?"

Probably not odd for Jeremy's mother. Probably not odd for someone used to having her every word obeyed.

I shrug. "I guess she just hoped that if she'd already bought the tickets, Jeremy wouldn't refuse."

"Well"—she sighs—"you can tell him tomorrow."

"No way. He'd be less likely to freak out if you tell him."

She hides her face again. "Oh, why did I start this?"

"Because you care, Mom. Look, how about this? You serve another of his favorites for dinner tomorrow night, and afterward, we'll tell him together."

five

My mom doesn't get a chance to cook that butter-him-up dinner for Jeremy. He's the one who answers the door when the FedEx man knocks just after lunch. One glance at the overnight delivery envelope, and I know what's coming. His jaw tightens when he reads the return address. My mom and I exchange a look and then watch in silence as he tears open the envelope and pulls out the airline tickets.

"Bloody hell."

My mom catches my eye and nods toward Jeremy.

"What is it?" I say, but when his eyes meet mine, they're saying I waited too long to ask the question.

"You knew." He looks from me to my mom and back to me. "Bloody fucking hell."

My mom heads to the kitchen before I can ask her to. "I had nothing to do with this, Jeremy. Your mother told Mom she'd already bought the tickets."

"Your mom?" With a sigh, he closes his eyes and shakes his head for a moment. "The phone call last night." He throws the tickets and envelope on the floor. "I will not be manipulated like this. I am not at their beck and call."

This is not the time to correct him on the timing of his mother's phone calls. "They just want to meet me and my mom. That's normal."

His eyes bulge, and he throws his hands in the air as he makes some unintelligible sound.

"Don't be unreasonable, Jeremy."

By the look he gives me, you'd think I suddenly sprouted six more heads and a tail.

He starts pacing the floor. "You … I can't … impossible to …"

Impossible to finish a sentence? He whirls toward me. I freak for a second, sure that I slipped and said that out loud, but then he just shakes his head and goes back to pacing. I've never seen Jeremy this mad. Not even when I accidentally told a roomful of writers he was my fiancé—six weeks before he proposed!

For once, I keep my mouth shut and wait out the storm.

After several minutes of pacing, he stops in front of one of the windows and stands there looking out. His jaw moves as though he's talking, but I don't hear anything. He turns toward me and smiles.

"None of this matters," he says calmly. "We're not going to London."

"Well, I'm going. And so is my mom. Your mother invited us."

"You will not."

"I'm sorry, but you seem to be under the illusion that you're my boss."

"I'm your fiancé. And they are my parents."

"Great. So you can introduce me to them in two weeks."

He stands rigid, looking straight into my eyes without blinking. I can't read a single thing from him.

"No need," he says.

"What does that mean?"

Jeremy stalks to the front door, pausing like a drama queen before he declares, "The wedding is off!"

Like hell. "What's the call on the engagement, Mr. High Tea? Still on?"

His response is a growl, and then he slams the door behind him.

Sometimes, I swear he thinks we're characters in one of our novels.

My mom peeks in from the hallway. "Is it safe to come out?"

"Yeah. He's gone." I flop down on the sofa. She moves my feet aside so she can sit at the other end.

"He doesn't really mean the wedding's canceled, sweetie."

"Oh, I know." She tries hard to give Jeremy and me privacy, but I'm sure our argument carried through the whole house. "Do you think we should give up the idea of going to London?"

"Well …" She pats my leg twice before folding her hands in her lap. She delays her answer even longer by sighing.

"So you do think we should forget it."

"No, of course not. I suggested the trip. I was just trying to remember if I heard his sister mention their parents when she was here last fall."

"Laura's not the one who has a problem with them. Apparently, they adore her."

"She is sweet, isn't she?"

"Mom."

"What? Was she just putting on an act when I was around?"

I sit up, hugging my knees. "You're insinuating Jeremy isn't sweet, and that's why his parents hate him."

"Oh, for goodness' sake. You know I didn't mean any such thing. I love Jeremy like he was my own."

The way she sides with him so often makes me wonder if she loves him better than her own. Better than her only daughter, at least. "It just doesn't seem right to marry him without knowing more about his family."

"It does seem odd that he's adamant you shouldn't meet them."

Ah-ha. My mom's suspicious too. I lean forward and grab her arm. "What do you think he's hiding?"

She blinks. "Hiding?"

I stand and start pacing the length of the living room, picking up the tickets along the way. "I've gone through a dozen scenarios. You know, I once considered that he was working undercover for the FBI or something."

"You what?"

"Or that he was some kind of criminal. Maybe a mobster. Maybe in the witness protection program."

"But … why?"

My mother is staring at me like I'm insane. Clearly I didn't inherit my imagination gene from her. I return to the sofa.

"For one thing, he didn't appear to have a job—that was before I knew he was a writer. And he was so secretive."

"But … you hadn't even met him then. How could you tell he was secretive?"

"I …" Why does she always try to confuse me? "Just trust me. Gabi thought so too."

She sighs. "If you hadn't spoken to him, sweetie, how could he tell you anything about himself?"

"Well … we had spoken."

"More than saying hello?"

I jump up and start pacing again. "The point is … he's not telling me everything now."

"And you've—"

"Yes, Mom, I've asked. He says his parents don't care about him, so why should I meet them."

"Well, obviously, it's not true that they don't care. Why else would they pay for us all to come to London?"

I stop dead. "That's true. So that's not the reason he doesn't want to go." I stare at the door Jeremy slammed as I consider possibilities. Then it hits me. I trudge back to the sofa, sink beside her, and lean my head on her shoulder. "I think I know why."

Our room is glowing neon red from the sunset, and Jeremy's still not home. But that's okay. I can't talk about the London trip yet. I'm not ready to hear him tell me the truth. For hours, I've sat here on our bed with the TV on, but I wouldn't be able to name a single program that came on if you paid me. I've been trying to deny the real reason he doesn't want me to meet his parents by thinking up others.

Reason number one—his parents object to me only because I'm American. No, that's stupid. Okay. Reason number two—it has to be because I'm not Alison. He said they expected him to marry her. It was practically an arranged marriage, right? So they're furious about him not marrying her. That's why he doesn't want me to meet them. He's just protecting my feelings.

I really, really want to believe that one. But would his mother pay for me to come there just so they could tell me in person how much they hate me? Still, I hold on to reason number two for a while on the chance that it's true they hate Jeremy and might get off on humiliating both of us at once.

But that third reason keeps screaming at me. I've pushed it away a zillion times, but it keeps coming back. What if the real reason—I jump when the door opens.

Jeremy slinks in. I turn off the TV but stay on the bed. He stops at the foot of it, head down and hands shoved deep in his jeans pockets.

"I'm sorry for overreacting," he says. "I already apologized to Marie." His head snaps up. "Not that she's more important than you, but she was in the living room when I came in."

Let my suspicion be wrong. Please, please, please let it be wrong.

"Say something, Chelsea."

"Did my mom accept your apology?"

"Yes."

"Okay."

He cocks his head, puzzled. "Does that mean you do too?"

"Is the wedding still on?"

"Of course it is. I love you."

"Okay."

He sighs. Just a normal sigh of relief. But for some reason I can't explain, it ticks me off. Big time. "How do you feel about a wedding in the back yard?"

"In your mother's back garden?"

"No, I thought we'd pick some random stranger's yard."

His right eyebrow arches, and he stares at me for a

moment before he gives me a half smile. "I thought you had your heart set on the beach?"

"Yeah, well, you don't want all that wind and sand, not that you had the guts to tell me that."

A frown cuts a deep crease between his brows, and he moves toward me, but I shoot him a look that stops him. He finger combs both hands through his hair as though he's going to put it in a tail and then holds them there as he studies me.

"Apparently, I've misinterpreted something," he says slowly. "You're still angry."

"Are you really planning to marry me?" There. I said it.

His mouth gapes, and his hands drop to his sides.

He's shocked that I figured him out. "That's why you don't want me to meet your parents, isn't it?"

"What?"

"If you'd married Alison, you would have been totally involved in all the wedding plans, right?"

He scoffs. "If I'd married her—which I never intended to do—I would have been lucky if she'd remembered to tell me the date and location."

"But your parents would have been thrilled to have her for a daughter-in-law."

"Why are we talking about Alison, for God's sake?" Suddenly, his face slackens. "Chelsea … have you changed your mind about marrying?"

"You're just using me, aren't you? And when you've had enough of slumming, you'll go back to England and marry her or some other upper-class woman like her."

The ring on my left hand feels like it weighs far more than three-carats of diamonds and a circlet of gold should. I'm trying to wriggle it off when he lunges forward.

"Don't you dare." He pulls me off the bed and into his arms.

In seconds, I'm a quivering blob of tears. Every time he tells me he loves me, I cry harder. He probably thinks I'm insane. Probably I am.

Twilight darkens our room before I get myself calmed down. If he wasn't holding me so tight, I'd be a puddle on the floor.

"Now," he says, "you're going to tell me what's really going on."

I pry Jeremy's arms loose. I need a minute, so I turn on the bedside lamp and grab a tissue to dry my eyes and blow my nose. He loves me ... so he says. He's really going to marry me ... so he says.

"Chelsea ..." He turns me back toward him and lifts my chin so I have to look at him.

Oh, hell. I might as well just face it. "You're ashamed of me, aren't you? That's the real reason you don't want me to meet your parents."

He closes his eyes.

Oh, God. I was right. My breath comes in quick, tiny, cold puffs. I try to move away, but he grabs me by the throat with both hands.

"You"—he smiles as he pretends to strangle me—"have gone completely around the bend." He moves his hands to my waist and pulls me into a kiss. "How could I ever be ashamed of you?"

"That's not the reason you don't want me to meet your parents?"

"I assure you it's not."

"Then why?"

He looks away from me. "We don't get on well. I told you that."

"So they don't approve of you being a writer. You're still their son. Their firstborn. And you're getting married. That's major. And Mom said your mother asked a lot of questions about us and the wedding, so that doesn't sound like she's not interested in you."

He says nothing. And he won't look at me either. Crap. He is hiding something. What, what, what? And just like that it comes to me.

"Have you been married before? That's what you're afraid I'll find out, isn't it? Ohmygod. You have a child?"

Okay, judging by his bugged-out eyes, I've reinforced that "around the bend" thing. He starts laughing.

When he catches his breath, he says, "Dear God. You'll imagine me an ex-con before long. A prison escapee even."

I'm struggling to look innocent of ever imagining any such thing whatsoever. "Don't be ridiculous. But you didn't answer my questions."

Jeremy's eyes say he's doubting I'm serious, so I ask again. "Have you ever been married and do you have—"

"Of course not. No ex-wife. No children. How can you think I wouldn't have told you those things by now?"

"Seriously? There's a lot you haven't told me about your life."

"Not really. And there's certainly nothing crucial I haven't told you. Well, all right. Here's something. I'm an ex-smoker. I started when I was twelve and quit … well, not quite a year ago."

"I already guessed that from the way you hold a pen when you're reading."

"Do I?" He glances at his right hand. "I still miss it."

"That's not the kind of thing I meant anyway."

"But that's my point. I've not hidden anything of importance from you."

"Then why aren't we going to—"

He presses his fingers to my lips and heaves a huge sigh. "Though I'm certain little good can come of it, and you'll likely be quite disappointed with my parents … we'll go to London."

I leap into his arms and wrap my legs around his waist while I kiss him long and hard. When I try to get down, he squeezes me tighter. "Let me down. I want to tell Mom."

"She knows."

"You told her before me?"

"Didn't you hear me say I saw her on my way to our room?"

"Wait. So you'd already made up your mind to go?" He says nothing. "You let me go through all that … that angst and crying for nothing?"

There go the eyebrows.

"Are you forgetting that you distracted me with wedding questions and then went totally mental and started on about Alison?"

Well, okay. I did. "Doesn't matter. Thank you for agreeing to go." I give him another kiss and try to wiggle out of his grasp.

"Hold on," he says. "I think I deserve make-up sex."

"Deserve?" I smack his shoulder, but I'm only teasing. I'm all for making up.

Jeremy and I both missed dinner, so after we *make up*, we head to Arturo's for street tacos. We drive through a brief shower, and I flash back to the first night we came here. He reaches across the console to take my hand. I wonder if he's remembering the same night. It's amazing how much my life has changed in seven months—well, his too. It's hard to believe that this time last year we didn't know each other existed.

"Oh, it just occurred to me," he says. "Will you be able to get a passport before we're meant to leave?"

I consider lying for a second, but my good side wins. "I already have one."

He frowns at me. "You told me you didn't."

"Well, that was true then, but I applied for one after we got engaged."

"I never had a chance of convincing you we didn't need to go to London, did I?"

"Nope."

"Is there anything else you've already decided for me?"

"Nothing we need to discuss right now."

One arched brow.

"I'm joking. I know how sensitive you are about having decisions made for you." (His father deciding Jeremy's career as a lawyer is the source of that touchiness.) "I have to figure out what to pack. What will the weather there be like in March?"

"Colder than it ever is here."

"Yikes." I consider my clothing choices. Then I think about Jeremy's clothes. In general, our ideas of appropriate attire are a few steps apart. I'll borrow some of Gabi's outfits. Her style is much closer to Jeremy's. More sophisticated. More adult, my mother would say. Definitely more what his parents would expect. And she can't wear them while she's pregnant anyway.

"I know what you're thinking, Chelsea. Just be yourself."

When he reads my mind like that, it always freaks me out. "I'd like to impress your parents, if you don't mind. And won't I need a nicer outfit or two?"

"I suppose … for when we have to have dinner with them."

"I'll talk to Laura. You don't know about women's clothes."

"I know you look sexy in anything."

"And that's how you want me to look when I meet your father?"

"Good God. I can't imagine a more disturbing question."

"Relax, High Tea. I'll make you proud."

He parks the car and comes around to open my door. He's gallant that way, and I allow it because I know there's not a sexist bone in his body—though sometimes you can't tell by the things he says. When I get out of the car, he surprises me by grabbing me by the shoulders.

"I'm always proud of you. And I'm serious about you not putting on an act for my parents … or anyone."

"You might want to rethink that, dude. I can remember a few times when you got your panties in a twist over something I did or said when I was being myself." I can almost see his brain flipping through our past.

He nods. "Fair enough. Think before you speak. Or act."

We order our tacos, and since the sky's clear here, we decide to eat at one of the patio tables set up outside the taco stand. We don't speak until we've each eaten half of our first taco.

"Do you remember the first time we ate these together?" Jeremy says.

"Of course."

"Why did you run out on me that night?"

"I don't remem—"

"Yes, you do," he says. "You must."

Sigh. "I was stupid." He's waiting for a better answer. "Okay. I thought you were using me to get to Gabi."

He stops the taco halfway to his open mouth and stares at me for a moment before closing his eyes and shaking his head. "That's not stupid. That's astoundingly demented. Even if we ignore the fact that she and Matt were engaged at the time, I'd already met Gabi. I'd lunched with her, talked to her on the phone, so why would I need to go through you?"

"I was drunk?"

"As I recall, you drank half of one beer."

I take a sip of my soda. "You've never really said why you don't get along with your brother."

He was about to take a bite but stops. "Seriously? I thought we'd agreed to stop the diversion tactics."

"Yeah. So answer my question. Why don't you get along with—"

"Hold on. Choose one: it's too embarrassing or painful or ridiculous to discuss."

"Huh?"

"Isn't one of those the reason you changed the subject?"

My eyes roll before I can stop them. "Never mind."

"So, which is it?"

Crap. Why can't he let it go? "It's embarrassing because it seems ridiculous, now, but it was painful at the time."

He laughs. "Impressive."

"Moving on."

"No. I still don't understand how in the midst of our first real conversation, which I thought was going quite well, you were sitting there thinking I was only interested in Gabi."

"Our food's getting cold."

That shuts him up, and we finish our dinner without any more conversation.

"Right," he says as soon as we're back in the car. "You can respond now."

"Geez. What does it matter now?"

He keeps his eyes on the road but motions with his hand for me to continue.

Sigh. "Isn't it obvious?"

"Not at all. At the time, I thought it had to be something I said, but the next day, you assured me it wasn't."

"It was me, Jeremy." He's quiet for a moment, but just when I think he's letting it go, he pulls to the curb and turns to me.

"Did you think you'd offended me in some way?"

He's serious about this.

"No. The truth is, I told myself I was stupid for assuming you were interested in me."

He laughs. A real belly laugh. Not exactly the sensitive reaction I'd hoped for.

"Thanks a lot. This is why I don't tell you what—" He shuts me up with a kiss.

"I'm sorry," he says. "I laughed because I spent the rest of that night thinking I'd been stupid for hoping you were interested in me."

"Really?"

"Yes."

"Well, I'm glad we got that straightened out."

♥ ♥ ♥

The last two weeks have been a blur. We launched our fourth book ten days ago, but we haven't made much progress on the next one—well, *I* haven't. Jeremy's been typing like mad, sometimes while looking at one of his journals, which I guess contains notes he made for our next book. (I've learned not to ask to read something before he's ready for me to see it.)

Gabi helped me raid her closet. And I told her to revise the wedding location to my mom's back yard—Jeremy and I will say our vows on the rose garden patio—so now Gabi can order the invitations. The smaller venue also means scaling back the guest list to only close friends and family, and it also solves the problem of which friends or family members to choose for bridesmaids and groomsmen. We'll have only our best friends; Gabi will stand with me and Ethan with Jeremy. Also that means there's no need for a rehearsal dinner, but we've asked Luisa to cater the wedding dinner. No wedding dress decision yet, but I promised Gabi I'll make up my mind as soon as we get back from London. And because I'm going to be one of her birth coaches, I made her promise not to have the baby while I'm gone.

This morning, I went to the salon to ditch the platinum and purple. I had my hair colored a natural blonde shade, and it's styled more … adult. It's totally boring, but I think it will go over better with Jeremy's parents. My mom and Jeremy are eating lunch when I get home.

"What do you think?" I ask, though by the way they're both staring at me the answer's pretty obvious.

"It's … nice," Mom says. "I'd forgotten what you looked like with your natural color."

"Thanks, Mom. Jeremy?"

"You look totally different."

"I made you a sandwich," she says. "It's on the counter."

Okay. So he doesn't like my hair. But he'll have to agree it looks more sophisticated. And it goes much better with the outfits Gabi loaned me. My mom keeps the lunchtime conversation going, apologetically asking if we might fit in a few touristy things during our trip. Jeremy, gracious as always, ensures her he and Laura will be happy to take us wherever we'd like to go.

After lunch, he excuses himself to go to our office, so I follow. We take our usual places, and he starts typing something almost immediately. I open my laptop to check our email and sales stats. But that's all the intention I have of working today. I'm waiting for Jeremy to say what's on his mind. About fifteen minutes later, he gets up and walks out of the room.

I open my laptop again and read through my packing list for the hundredth time. I just know I'll forget something major. Jeremy prefers to pack his own things, and he never forgets anything, but I always end up with a full suitcase lacking a top or a pair of earrings or shoes I meant to bring— sometimes all three. I glance up when Jeremy comes in and then go back to my list. Five seconds later, just when he sets back down at his desk, it hits me.

"You shaved your beard!"

"Aren't you the observant one."

"Why?"

He swivels his chair toward me. "I thought it appropriate."

"Huh?"

"I have an appointment to get my hair cut later this afternoon."

"No." I jump off the bed. "Don't you dare."

"It's my hair."

"But I love it long."

For a moment, he only looks me in the eye. "But wouldn't it impress my parents if I looked the way they expect me to?"

"Oh."

"Precisely."

I touch my hair. "Does it look that bad?"

"It doesn't look bad at all. It just doesn't look like you."

"But it will look bet—" Oops, he probably won't like the clothes I've packed either. "I don't have time to change it back."

The look he gives me says he knows that's exactly why I waited until the day before we leave to do it. I go sit on his lap. I rub my fingers across his smooth jaw. His beard was the sexy designer-stubble kind, so it will grow back in a week.

"You're still sexy," I say.

"And?"

"I'm sorry I didn't ask you—"

"Bloody hell, Chelsea!" In a single motion, he sets me on my feet and stands. "That's not what angered me. I hate that you're not being yourself."

"Of course I am."

He couldn't look more incredulous. "Thinking I expect you to ask my permission to change your hair is normal for our relationship?"

"You're right. Okay, dude, so this is my new look. Deal with it."

He rubs both hands down his face, but I think that's mostly to hide his smile.

six

It's Friday evening, and we've landed and gone through customs and passport control at Heathrow Airport. I totally can't believe this is finally happening. At first, I didn't trust Jeremy's explanation for the odd flight times his mother scheduled for us. We left LA at midnight and got to our hotel in New York early yesterday morning. We went to sleep in the afternoon so we could wake up in time for our flight to London. Jeremy's mother was thoughtful enough to book an overnight stay in New York so we wouldn't have to fly straight through from LA to London. (*Ohmygod* you wouldn't believe the hotel she picked.)

Here in London, we'll stay with Laura. I won't be meeting their parents until Sunday. Jeremy made some lame comment about needing to acclimate first—like London's on another planet or something, but I let that go because I love being with Laura. Besides, we have sixteen days here, so I'm sure we'll visit with them a few times.

Our combined luggage is stacked on two carts—that's "trolleys" to Jeremy. I'm pushing one as Mom and me follow him out to the line of waiting taxis. A driver opens the doors and shepherds her and me into the backseat. I can't understand a word the driver is saying, but Jeremy doesn't have that problem. Soon, the luggage is loaded, and we're off.

While my mom interrogates Jeremy about a million different things, I'm trying to take in as much of the city as I can on the drive from the airport to Laura's, which isn't much from the freeway because it's already dark. London is smaller than LA in area—I looked it up—but the traffic certainly seems as heavy. It's a longer drive than I expected, twenty-five minutes so far, but we finally exit into a residential area. In the next short distance, we pass several little parks, and in between those are dense neighborhoods. From what I can see by streetlights, most of the houses are tall, skinny, and squished together—row houses—some brick, some stone, and on some of the streets, each house in the row is painted a different pastel color. They kind of remind me of San Francisco's Victorian "painted ladies." Wait. Duh. This is where everything Victorian originated. I have to keep reminding myself London is, like, ancient.

Jeremy laughs at something my mom said. He can try to deny it, but he's excited to be in London again, and even if his mood darkens when we see his parents, at least he'll be happy for the first forty-eight hours we'll have alone with Laura.

I'm looking the opposite way when the taxi pulls to the curb, so I don't get my first view of Laura's house until I get out. "Hey, this looks like where you used to live."

Jeremy gives me a puzzled look as he helps my mother from the car. Uh-oh. Back when I was sort of stalking him, I looked up his Notting Hill address on Google Maps street view, but that's not one of the things I confessed to him. We've been in England for less than three hours, and already

I've forgotten to think before I speak. While Jeremy's paying the driver, he's still looking a question at me.

"I meant it looks like I imagined your place looked."

"This is where I used to live," he says as he and the driver unload our luggage. "I sold it to Laura."

"Why didn't you tell me that?" (Isn't it amazing how I can excuse my own lapses in confession but not his?) He doesn't get a chance to answer my question because Laura's door flies open.

"You're here," she cries as she runs out to hug us all. "I'm so excited you're staying with me. We'll have loads of fun."

Laura gives my hair a curious glance but doesn't comment. Like a magazine ad come to life, she's a beautiful blue-eyed blonde with perfect skin. And though I've learned she's always up for some fun, she's all poise and class on the outside. I'm all … well, clumsy and quirky—inside and out. So I'm sure she's wondering why our hair color is now a pretty close match.

Everyone grabs a bag or two—three for Jeremy—and we parade inside.

In the entry, Laura lets go of the bag she wheeled in. "Ladies, come have a welcome drink with me. Jeremy, carry yours and Chelsea's bags up top, and put Marie's in the guest room."

"Yes, missus. When I finish this chore, I'll hurry back to the scullery and polish all the silver, I will."

"Always the arse-kisser, aren't you, Jemmy?"

"Jemmy?" I say.

She smirks. He growls.

"I'll help you," my mom tells Jeremy.

"No need, Marie, but thank you." He starts up the stairs with the first load.

Laura leads us into the living room. Wow. It's gorgeous. Mostly taupe and white, with an incredible and elegantly aged oriental carpet in shades of blue and tan over bleached wood floors. A perfect combination of contemporary and tradi- tional. It's the kind of room you see in movies and interior design magazines.

"Make yourself comfortable," she says. "Wine or some- thing harder?"

"What do you usually drink, Laura?" my mom asks. "Not that I assume you drink every afternoon."

"I do, always," Laura says with a soft laugh. "Gin and tonic."

"That will be fine for us too, won't it, Chelsea?"

"What? Oh. Sure." Not that I've ever tasted a gin and tonic, but I'm game. I drop into the nearest armchair, a gor- geous white leather one. My mom settles on the sofa, which I'd bet cost more than all her living room furniture combined. I'm taking in every inch of the room. This isn't the bachelor "flat" I pictured when Jeremy told me he'd sold it.

It sounds like he's on his second trip to the bedrooms. I can't wait to see the rest of these rooms, but I'm feeling guilty about that excitement. If he hadn't met me, he wouldn't have had to give up this beautiful place.

Jeremy joins us just as Laura hands me my drink. He pours himself something brown—Scotch I presume—but all of Laura's liquor is in decanters, so it's hard to tell.

"You've redecorated the bedrooms," he says to Laura.

"Actually, I decorated the bedrooms. You never quite got around to doing that. Or was that bare white walls and hap- hazard furniture arrangement strewn with clothes your idea of style?"

"Jeremy was a slob?" pops out of both my mom's mouth and mine simultaneously.

Laura looks at each of us and then at Jeremy.

Jeremy points at her. "Be fair, Lolly, or I'll tell them about the—"

"All right, he wasn't that bad." She gives him a smirk. "And to be completely fair, he didn't live here long enough to finish all he'd planned to do." Gracefully, she sweeps the hand holding her drink, gesturing to the room. "This is all Jeremy's work."

My eyes and mouth go all googly. Though I lived in his apartment, he'd told me he furnished it through a rental company, so when we were moving and he packed up the high-end decorative items, I just assumed he'd had to buy those from the company. Dang. No wonder he'd rather live in my mother's nice house than in the kind of apartment we could afford, filled with my crappy furniture.

My mother doesn't seem surprised. "You have wonderful taste, Jeremy."

"Thank you, Marie." Jeremy moves toward the distressed brown leather club chair and, with a finger under my chin, closes my gaping mouth as he passes. "Drink up, Chelsea."

I take a gulp and nearly choke. Gin and tonic is totally not my thing. It tastes like my father's aftershave smelled. I glance at Jeremy. He's barely hiding his amusement. He knew I wouldn't like it. Silly man; he should know by now that I'll get him back eventually.

"Do you play well, Laura?" My mom is pointing to the piano at the far end of the room in front of the bay window.

"Oh"—she and Jeremy exchange a look—"no ... um ... it's for looks."

I'm not sure what that was all about. Did she think Jeremy had told us she was a concert pianist or something?

"I made reservations for dinner," Laura says, "but if you're not up for that, I could fix a light meal here. I know it takes a while to adjust to the time change."

"I think we're fine for dinner." Jeremy looks to me and my mom to see if we disagree. We don't.

"Good." Laura glances at the clock on the wall to her left. "We'll leave at a quarter till. So. Was your flight uneventful?"

"It was very nice," my mom says. "No problems at all. And since your mother was kind enough to plan an overnight stay in New York, that's helped us to adjust to the time change."

"Well, I remember from my short visit last fall that you dine earlier in the evening, so I hoped it would still feel early to you when you arrived." Laura sips her drink and then turns to Jeremy. "I read the new book. Adored it." She looks at me then back at Jeremy with a devilish smile. "Which of you wrote those knickers-melting sex scenes?"

My mom shoots to her feet. "Excuse me, but where's the …"

"Oh," Laura says, "we passed the guest loo in the hall, just round the corner."

We're all silent as my mother leaves the room, and then Laura speaks again.

"I embarrassed her, didn't I? She's such a dear."

"No problem," I say. "She's just sensitive about that topic with Jeremy in the room."

"To answer your question," he says, "Chelsea did. For the rest, I wrote from the hero's point of view, and Chelsea wrote all the heroine's."

Laura nods. "I figured. The heroines are stronger now.

And the love scenes have definitely improved since your first book."

"I thought Wanting More was hot," I say in Jeremy's defense.

"Well, yes, but these new books have added an emotional element to the sex, which makes them hotter." Laura gets up to take hers and Jeremy's glasses to the bar. "So the next one is another California romance?"

"Yes," Jeremy says. "The last."

Laura's eyes widen. She looks at me. "The last Penny James novel?"

"No," I say, "just the last of the California series. At least for now."

"So what's after?"

I'll let Jeremy answer. I still haven't shared my idea with him.

"Well … we haven't discussed it much, but Chelsea will make that call. She has better instincts, and she understands the market more than I."

Wait, what? What he just said is news to me. "What do you mean, I'm making the call?"

He gives me a look I can't discern. "Aren't you the boss?"

"Chelsea's the boss?"

My mom is back. "Geez, Mom, you don't have to sound like that would be a total disaster."

She responds with a wide-eyed questioning look.

"Mom."

Smiling, she reclaims her spot on the sofa. "I'm just teasing you, sweetie. If Jeremy wants to let you wear the pants in your relationship, it's none of my business."

"We were talking about our writing, Marie."

She turns to Jeremy. "Do you really think she's capable?"

I huff a sigh and swig my drink, totally forgetting I hate it. The shock of the taste dilutes my irritation. There's no use trying to explain—for the hundredth time—that I've progressed to doing half the writing.

"A refill, Marie?" Laura hands back Jeremy's glass.

"Yes, please."

Laura takes my mother's glass and reaches for mine. "What would you actually like this time, Chelsea?"

"Sorry." I hand her my barely touched glass. "But I'm good."

She frowns. "Are you sure?"

Oh, crap. Have I insulted her? I glance at Jeremy.

"She'll have a tequila and lime," he says.

"Perfect." Laura's smile is back, and a minute later, we're all drinking again. We chat until it's time to go to dinner. She tells Jeremy to show us our rooms in case we'd like to freshen up. I'm wondering if this means we should change clothes and hoping Jeremy's good taste extends to knowing that.

"How should we dress?" my mom asks Laura.

"You're fine," she says. "It's casual." She looks at Jeremy. "Catalano's?"

"Ah, yes. This way to the bedrooms, ladies."

He leads the way back toward the entry but then motions for my mother and me to go ahead up the stairs. I know from past experience that he does this from his innate sense of gallantry. He's the brave knight, ready to break our fall should one or both of us fair maidens tumble down the stairs. Isn't he cute?

The upstairs decor does not disappoint. Apparently, excellent taste runs in the Pearce family. I get a glimpse of the guest room when Jeremy opens the door for my mother. Pale tan walls, bleached wood floors, and muted aquas in bedding and drapes. Very peaceful. Beachy.

Jeremy waits for me to start up another flight of stairs.

"So up top means the third floor," I say.

"Second."

I glance down the stairs behind us. "But isn't that the second floor."

"In England, that's the first."

"And where we had drinks?"

"The ground floor. And the kitchen and garden are on the lower ground floor."

"Makes no sense to me, but okay."

He opens the door to a huge loft room. It's painted pale cream, and the flooring is some dark wood. There's a sloped ceiling on one side, a sitting area in the center, and a bed beyond that. At each end are dormer windows. In front of one of these, on the street side, sits a massive desk.

"You wrote Wanting More in this room, didn't you?"

"I rewrote it here, but how did you know?"

"I just feel it."

"My little witch." He takes me in his arms and kisses me like we're not expected to be downstairs in ten minutes.

"Save that for later." I wiggle out of his grasp. "Are you sure I'm dressed all right for dinner?"

"You look perfect to me." He reaches for me again.

"Forget it." I look around for our suitcases. "Maybe I should wear something else."

Jeremy sighs. "Laura is wearing jeans."

"And she looks dressed up no matter what she wears."

"Are you dressed well enough for Mama Mia's?"

"Yes, but—"

"Same kind of restaurant."

"Okay. But I want to check my hair and makeup."

He points to a door in the corner. "The bathroom up here is nice but small."

It's more than nice and not so small at all. God, he must miss this place.

Catalano's is *not* the same as Mama Mia's. It's definitely upscale Italian. We're shown to a table set for five, and when the hostess doesn't remove the extra place setting, Jeremy tenses.

"Who's joining us, Laura?"

"You'll see." She smiles and holds out the wine list to him. He frowns at her for a moment before he takes it.

The wine Jeremy orders is so fine, I don't even want to think about how much it costs. I almost choke on my second sip when someone comes up behind us and slaps Jeremy on the back.

"Ethan!" Jeremy cries out. He rises for a man hug. "You said you'd be out of town until Tuesday."

Ethan shrugs. "I lied."

The first time I saw Ethan on Skype, I was surprised that didn't look anything like I'd pictured him—well, that's because Jeremy used his best friend's name when he wrote his first romance, so after he told me that, I pictured the real Ethan the way Jeremy described the character in the book. But the fictional Ethan has blond hair and the real Ethan has curly black hair. But what I couldn't see clearly on screen was that he has the most amazing eyes—they're golden. And they're looking expectantly into mine right now. Uh-oh. I think he's just said something to me.

"Hi," I say. "It's nice to see you in real life." (Could that sound any lamer?)

Ethan grins and grabs me in a hug. "I'd wager you'll take that back before this night is over."

Jeremy introduces him to my mom. "My goodness," she says, "you and Jeremy must be the two most handsome young men in London."

Ethan bows. "And it's easy to see that your beautiful daughter takes after you."

My mom giggles. Ethan squeezes Laura's shoulders as he passes behind her to take his place between her and my mom.

So now our party looks like four young people and their mother, but somehow my mom always seems to fit in—unless someone mentions sex. Actually, that's not true. It's just when Jeremy's around that she acts like a prude. She may never get over her embarrassment the moment she realized the sex scenes she'd just been gushing about were written by him. Freaked her out big time.

The appetizer arrives along with another bottle of wine. A minute later, I revise my first opinion of Catalano's. This restaurant looks nicer, but if the appetizer is any indication, the food is not as good as Luisa's. I do love this wine though. I breathe it in, quietly swish it around my mouth, swallow, and note the finish. With my limited knowledge, I can't identify the varietal, but I'm pretty sure I detect cherry and oak and maybe—

Jeremy slams his hand on the table. "Stop right there, Ethan!"

What the hell? Ethan's glaring at Jeremy, and my mom's the picture of shock. With my mind on the wine, I lost track of the conversation.

"I'm only telling the truth," Ethan says.

"Rubbish. You're telling your cocked-up version of the truth."

"You can't deny it, Jeremy," Laura says. "Half of West London knew about you."

Crap. Please, someone say something to clue me in.

Jeremy lays a hand over mine. "Don't believe a word of this, Chelsea."

"Oh. Okay. I won't."

Everyone bursts out laughing, including Jeremy.

"What's going on?"

Jeremy wraps an arm around my shoulders and kisses my cheek.

"Daydreamer's prank," Laura explains. "Ethan and Jeremy used to pull it on anyone whose attention wandered."

"That was hilarious," my mom says.

"Forgive us, Chelsea?" Ethan asks.

"Yes. And as much as I hate to, I have to admit that was funny. I can only imagine what life here with you two was like."

"It was horrid," Laura says, "just horrid."

The gleam in her eyes says she doesn't mean that at all.

The rest of dinner is prankless, and the food turns out to be better than I anticipated. Afterward, we walk a few blocks through a small park to a pub Jeremy, Ethan, and Laura seem to know well. Listening to them talk is entertaining in itself. Jeremy's accent has grown stronger since we arrived in London, and they're all using slang I'm not familiar with. A couple of times I totally miss the point of what they're saying, but I don't feel offended or excluded because I'm sure they don't even realize they're doing it. It's just normal speech to them. But a tiny part of me feels weird witnessing this different Jeremy.

seven

Considering where Laura lives and that it's Saturday morning, it's a no-brainer that we're walking the few blocks to the Portobello Road Market, but first we'll eat breakfast at a place they call Tabernacle.

Since I want to taste yummy things at the market stalls, I order just a croissant and juice, but Jeremy feeds me bites of his bacon and eggs because he worries I don't eat enough protein. Isn't he sweet?

Jeremy says the market runs for two miles, which makes our Front Street Market lame by comparison. "Will we see the whole thing today?"

"If you want," he says. "Just be careful who you're bumping into, Ms. Cole."

Laura frowns at his formality. "Ms. Cole?"

"One of our early meetings," he explains, "and the least injurious, I believe, was at the local farmers market. Chelsea sought to get my attention with an elbow to the solar plexus."

"I did not. That was an accident."

My mom pats my hand. "He's teasing you, sweetie."

It's totally possible to roll your eyes without moving them. I can only hope she doesn't ask me to try on some goofy craft clothing at this market.

After we finish eating, we head out to Portobello Road. By the time we've made our way slowly through six blocks of the market, I'm on sensory overload. There are just too many sights and sounds and smells. My dear attentive Jeremy sends Laura and my mom off after something and steers me to a quieter spot a few feet down a side street.

He brushes the hair out of my eyes and gives me a quick kiss. "Better? Your eyes were glazing over."

"Just give me a minute to recharge." He's massaging my shoulders when my mom and Laura, bearing gifts, join us. I reach for one of the sugary cakes, and Jeremy smacks my hand away. He gives me a warm cheese and sausage roll and takes the raspberry-colored juice drink for himself.

"You can have some of this juice after you eat your protein," he says.

"Yes, Daddy." I stick my tongue out at him.

He looks at Laura, shaking his head. "You think we should take her word that she's an adult or demand to see a certified birth record?"

I scarf down my roll as ordered, then reach for the juice bottle, but my brain goes blue screen, and I misjudge the location of my mouth. Most of the juice ends up on the front of my jacket—my white jacket. Three pairs of eyes stare at me in disbelief. Laura takes the bottle from my hand. My mom starts dabbing me with a napkin. Jeremy guffaws. I shoot him a deadly look, but that only makes him laugh more, so I kick him.

"Ow." He frowns at me, but he's struggling not to laugh again. "You have to admit that was—"

"Not funny, Jeremy. And why didn't you buy water instead of berry juice?"

"I assure you I would have if I'd known you were going to wear it." He hugs me—making sure his front doesn't actually touch mine. "I'm sorry for laughing. Be right back."

We watch him until he disappears from view on Portobello Road.

"We'll drop your jacket at the cleaners on the way home," Laura says.

"I'm sure they can get out the stain," my mom says.

"I'm still thirsty." I reach for the juice. For a second, Laura hesitates, and I wonder if she's going to hold it and just tip it up for me like I'm a toddler, but after a glance at my chest, she hands the bottle to me. Yeah, what can it matter if I spill it again?

A minute later, Jeremy sprints toward us with a lime-green scarf in hand. He wraps it around my neck, ties it under my chin, and tries to arrange the ends to hide the stain.

"You're strangling me." I loosen the knot. He's trying to help, so I stop myself from asking why he choose lime instead of purple or hot pink, which might have camouflaged the stain instead of calling attention to it.

He frowns as the ends of the scarf refuse to stay where he wants them to. "Well, I tried."

My mom pats his shoulder. "And it was an excellent try, dear."

"You just can't take me anywhere nice, right?" I smile and take his arm. "Let's go. There's more to see."

Okay, so London has a huge population, and even though it's not quite spring here, some of this crowd is bound to be tourists, so it was freaking me out that Jeremy keeps running into people he knows until I remembered this used to be his neighborhood. Besides "Jeremy," of course, he's been hailed as "Pearce" like men usually do, but the one I'll have to question him about is "Handsome One," which three guys have called him—and not in a flirting way. He *is* handsome, but there seems to be an inside joke there or something. Now, someone's called that out to him again.

I turn around to see who Jeremy's talking to, but my eyes never make it that far. They stop on a shop window. Specifically on a dress in that window. I've joked about things calling to me—a kick-ass pair of jeans, a chocolate éclair, Coachella tickets, for instance—but I never really felt that experience until now. That dress is calling my name. It's not a modern dress. I mean, duh, it's in the window of an antique shop, but it's sort of classic. Glamorous. Which is not a word I use often, but that's what comes to mind. It looks like it has two layers—a shimmery, transparent smoky lavender over an opaque lavender—and subtle beading, mostly on the bodice. I love that dress. But it's not like anything I've ever worn before. I mean, it's not me.

"It's you." Jeremy whispers in my ear.

"It is?"

"It has that thirties film-star vibe. You'd look smashing in it."

Smashing? I study his face for signs he's joking. No one's ever told me I reminded them one single bit of a thirties film star, not even my mom. "Are you serious?"

He opens his mouth to answer, but Laura, walking up beside us, interrupts him. "Are we captivated by that dress?"

"We are," Jeremy says.

"Oh, Chelsea. You must buy it."

"Where would I ever wear a dress like that?"

"Your wedding," my mom says from behind me.

I can't deny I was wondering about that possibility, but I'm surprised my mother is suggesting the same thing. "But it's not a real wedding dress, Mom."

"And you haven't liked any of the real wedding dresses Gabi has shown you."

"But it's not white."

"Oh yes, we must perpetuate that outmoded custom," Jeremy says.

"Yards and yards of white lace and tulle wouldn't suit you," Laura adds. "But this dress is gorgeous and chic. Come on then"—she grabs my arm—"let's go take a closer look."

The four of us squeeze into the small empty floor area of the antique shop.

"Welcome," says the man inside and offers Jeremy his hand. "Brian Woodridge, proprietor. How may I help you?"

"We're interested in that dress in the window," Laura tells him.

His eyes light up, and he turns to her. "That gown came in only yesterday. It's not original, I'm sorry to say. A replica of a 1937 Paris design."

"Good," I whisper to my mom, "it won't be too expensive."

Mr. Proprietor lifts the mannequin out of the window and turns it toward us. After a glance at my stained jacket, he shoots me a pointed look and pulls the mannequin back several inches. Message received. I pull out my phone and snap a photo.

"This gown was so beautifully preserved," he says, "I hesitated to expose it to daylight, but for this one day ..."

"Preserved?" I say. "But you said it was a replica."

"Indeed. This dress dates to 1962 and was created exclusively for the Princess Consort of Monaco."

My mother gasps. "Grace Kelly?"

"The one and only."

Crap. It belonged to some princess even my mom has heard of. There's no way I can afford this dress. I try to catch Jeremy's eye to signal him to get us out of this awkward situation, but he's watching Laura as she examines the fabric and beading.

"It's as though it were a bespoke design for you, my dear," Mr. Proprietor says to Laura. "You'll look as lovely in it as Princess Grace did."

Okay, then. Let Laura deal with him. I grab my mother's arm and take a step toward the door. She resists, frowning at me before turning her attention back to Woodridge. He's droning on about the beading detail.

"… art deco without being ostentatious. The bias-cut sheath is a luxurious grade of silk satin that we rarely see nowadays. It's scrumptious in hand and will beautifully grace the form."

Laura exchanges a look with Jeremy, and he cocks an eyebrow in question to me. Is he asking if Snooty Proprietor sounds like he's a designer competing on Project Runway? Jeremy certainly can't be asking if I agree about grades of silk. I shrug. He shoots back a quizzical frown.

Laura, who's observed our silent exchange, speaks. "Chelsea?"

I don't have any idea what she's asking either. Why am I the only one here who seems confused? I couldn't have missed more than a few words about the beading. Everyone's looking at me.

"It's … nice." That answer didn't come out the question I heard in my head, but it seems to satisfy everyone … well, except Snooty, who's looking at me like I insulted him. Jeremy nods to my mother, and she pulls me toward the door.

"What was that all about?" I ask her when we're outside.

"They're negotiating the price. Good job downplaying your interest. That low-key 'nice' should save us some money."

"Oh no!" I turn to go back into the shop, and she pulls me back. "They can't buy that dress, Mom."

"Oh yes, they can and will. You love it."

"A dress made for a princess will cost way too much. Kate Middleton's dress cost almost half a million!"

"Oh, don't be silly. That's completely different. And Jeremy knows what we can afford. You're going to look so beautiful, sweetie."

Jeremy scowls when I ask how much the dress cost. "Not a worry. It was well within the budget. I thought it best to have it shipped directly to our house, so you'll receive it soon after we're back home."

So, yay! I found the perfect wedding dress when I wasn't even looking for it. I sent the photo to Gabi, but with the time difference, she might not have seen it yet. She'll appreciate the style but probably freak that it's not a traditional white dress. But it's so beautiful, she'll come around. Oh, and I can change my hair to silver … ooh, with a lavender underlayer? Or maybe that would be too matchy-matchy. Contrast? Complement? And will I wear a regular veil? What did brides wear in the thirties? Mr. Proprietor mentioned art deco, so I should probably look for some jeweled headband or something, right? The perfect one could be right here in one of these stalls.

"Your mom looks tired," Jeremy whispers.

She does, and we still have to walk back to Laura's. So forget more shopping. We have next Saturday anyway. "Does anyone mind if we leave?"

"Fine with me," Laura says, and Mom nods. "Let's stop for tea on the way back to my house."

Tea really means a light meal—I've learned that much—and then we'll have dinner later this evening. We set off for Laura's house, stopping at the cleaners to drop off my jacket. It's warmer now, but I'm still cold in just my sweater and scarf, so I don't refuse Jeremy's jacket, even though I look stupid because it's miles too big for me. Just as I begin to recognize we're almost to Laura's house, she turns down another street.

Jeremy grabs her arm. "No ... not the café."

"Why?"

He flicks his eyes in my direction, obviously signaling something to Laura.

"Right," she says. "How about Monty's?"

We walk a block in the opposite direction to a pub called The Brendan Arms. I guess Monty is the owner. Again, this is one of those bright upscale pubs ... with prices to match. But if I mention that, I'll get another scowl from Jeremy. And since we've downscaled the wedding plans, I guess I shouldn't worry so much about money.

What's more important is all the secrets I sense Laura and Jeremy are keeping. It's like they have their own language, spoken mostly with just eyes, facial expressions, and gestures. I should be keeping notes on all the things I want to question Jeremy about when we're alone. Or better yet, I'll ask him in front of Laura, which is probably the best way to get the full story.

When Jeremy and Laura return from the bar with pints for me and him and gin and tonics for Mom and her, I plunge in. "So, Jeremy, who's at the café that you didn't want me to meet?" Yep, there goes the eye thing between them.

Jeremy opens his mouth, then closes it without saying anything. He takes a gulp of his beer.

"The owner's sister," Laura says.

"Thank you," Jeremy says sarcastically.

"Did it end badly?" I ask.

"The way Jeremy tells the story, it never began."

"It didn't," he says.

My mom pats Jeremy's hand. "Well, that's all in the past, isn't it? I'm sure Chelsea wouldn't like to be reminded of—"

"Mom!"

"You see, sweetie?"

Sigh. It will be impossible to get any dirt on Jeremy with my mom playing defense for him. Maybe I can get Laura alone and quiz her. Maybe she'll take me to the café, and I can get a look at this woman. My thoughts are interrupted by Ethan's arrival.

"I got texts from dozens of your devoted fans alerting me you were spotted at the market," he says to Jeremy.

"Sod off."

Ethan just laughs and pulls up a chair. "So, what are tonight's plans … dinner and dancing, dinner and bullfighting, dinner and a jewel heist?"

"I won't be making it for dinner even," my mom says. "Jet lag has caught up with me."

Concern creases Jeremy's forehead. "Are you not feeling well, Marie?"

"No, dear, I'm just tired. Really."

"They have delicious soups here," Laura tells her. "We'll order some to take away."

"That would be lovely. I noticed potato leek on the menu."

I'm not sure I buy the jet lag thing. I think Mom's just feeling like a fifth wheel, but once she makes up her mind about something like this, she won't budge.

When we finish our plates of appetizers, Laura goes to order the soup. Mom likes to have something sweet at the end of the day, so I get up to join Laura and add a dessert to that order. As I'm walking away from the table, my phone vibrates in my pocket. It's Gabi.

> **That dress is so YOU.**
> **You approve?**
> **Totally. Now I can shop for mine. Call me.**
> **Can't now. I will ASAP. Miss you.**
> **Same here. TTYL.**

Okay. So the wedding plans are back on track. Now, I only have to worry about getting Jeremy's parents to come.

It's quickly decided that we'll have Indian for dinner, but the battle between Jeremy, Laura, and Ethan over which restaurant takes a good fifteen minutes. Luckily, I'm exempt from offering an opinion. Finally, the decision is made—two to one —in favor of quality over ambience, with a promise to Ethan that he can choose where we'll go for drinks afterward.

We're halfway through the meal—which is the best Indian food I've ever had—when I say, "So. What's up with people calling you Handsome One like it's your name or title or something?"

"Nothing," Jeremy says, shooting a warning look at Ethan.

I look to Laura for an answer.

"Just … silliness." She takes a healthy swig of her plum wine cocktail.

I turn back to Jeremy. "Seriously? I'm about to marry you, and you're keeping secrets about nicknames?"

"You don't think he's handsome?" Ethan says.

"Of course I do, but—"

Jeremy waves a dismissive hand. "It's just silliness, like Laura said."

"But what's the joke?"

"No joke," Ethan says, "it's an identity. Crafted during our school days."

Jeremy's concentrating on his curry, but he looks up enough to glower at Ethan.

"What's your school nickname?" I ask Ethan.

"Charmer," Laura says. "Meaning he thinks he can charm himself out of any trouble."

"Or into any girl's knickers," Jeremy adds.

Ethan, taking both as compliments, grins and takes a sitting bow. His black curls seem permanently ruffled, one or two falling over his forehead, giving him an innocent boyish look that totally contrasts that devilish grin.

"Our Laura's called Posset," he says.

"Posset?"

"It's a lemon dessert," Jeremy explains. "Sweet and sour. Like she is."

"Heavy on the sour," Ethan says, and Laura jabs a knuckle into his bicep.

"Everyone in your group had a nickname?"

"You didn't do that?" Laura asks.

"Well … no. Not like that, I guess."

"Beach bunny," Jeremy mutters.

I nearly choke on a swig of beer. "Who the hell told you that?"

Jeremy's mouth drops open. "I … uh … maybe I got that wrong."

"That's an insult?" Laura says.

"I didn't know." Jeremy leans over and kisses my cheek. "Sorry."

"Right, then," Ethan says, "give us a clue, eh?"

They all look at me expectantly. "A beach bunny is a girl who hangs around surfers." They frown, so I clarify. "And sleeps with them."

"All of them?" Ethan says. "And individually or—"

Jeremy explodes. "For Christ's sake, Ethan."

"I wasn't implying that Chelsea—"

"I was one of them … a surfer, I mean. Not a beach bunny. I didn't—"

"Of course you didn't," Jeremy and Laura say together.

"None of them?" Ethan says.

Jeremy jumps to his feet.

Ethan holds up his hands. "I withdraw the question."

Jeremy sits, but his glare remains.

"Handsome One," Ethan taunts Jeremy.

Jeremy's eyes flash fire. Laura lowers her head and bites her lip. It takes me a second to catch on.

"Oh yeah?" I say to Jeremy. "That's what your nickname implies?"

"Means," Ethan clarifies.

"All in the past," Jeremy says.

Ethan shrugs. "A year gone maybe?"

Wow. I hope Jeremy never gives me the deadly look he's giving Ethan.

"Enough!" Laura holds out both palms, one in each guy's direction. "Let's not ruin this night with bloodshed between you two."

"Wouldn't be the first time," Jeremy mutters.

Ethan laughs. "Dear God, that night we drove your new car down to Brighton …"

I'm afraid to open my eyes. I don't want to wake up. But my backside is cold, which means Jeremy's already out of bed. Do the British have a higher alcohol tolerance or what? I'd swear my toenails are sore. My brain is totally scrambled. I can't remember even one full sentence spoken last night past dinner. I think harder. Nope. Just a swirling mass of words and music and faces—what the hell? At some point, was I arguing with some huge red-haired guy? Oh, *crap*. I think he was the bouncer.

When the bathroom door opens, I risk peeking through my lashes. Jeremy strides out, gloriously naked, and starts getting dressed.

"Hey," I croak.

"Good morning, sleepyhead."

"Did I get thrown out of a bar last night?"

He grins. "You did."

Groan. "Sorry."

"For what? It was hilarious."

"Hilarious?"

Jeremy zips up his jeans. "He asked you to get down off the table, and—"

"Ohmygod. Stop." It all comes back to me. I was standing on the table, but the red-haired guy stepping toward me was so tall the top of his head was almost level with my chin. He glared at me.

"All right, lass, down from the table with you."

"You can't bully me, you … bully."

He reached both hands toward my waist, but I backed up. "I'm only thinking of your safety, luv."

"If you lay a hand on me, you overgrown leprechaun, I'll rip your dick off and stuff it down your throat."

For a second, he froze, his face blanked with surprise. Then anger flamed his face, and he grabbed me with both hands. As he lifted me off the table, I planted a big sloppy kiss on his mouth.

Was the cheering for me or him? I didn't get a chance to find out because thirty seconds later I was standing outside the bar.

Groan. I pull the blanket over my head.

Jeremy pulls it off. "Sounds like you remembered. I thought you could hold your liquor better than that, Cole."

"Go away."

"You have to face the day sooner or later. And it's later. Take your shower."

Despite my groans and complaints that he's killing me, he pulls me out of bed and pushes me into the bathroom. The horror I'm faced with in the mirror nearly scares away my hangover. But hey, I entertained everyone last night. "Hilarious," he said. Sure. How long does it take to live down hilarious?

As I stand under the hot spray, bits of the conversation last night between Jeremy, Laura, and Ethan come back to me. The three of them reliving their past together. As close as triplets. Think how much of my life I've shared with friends, especially Gabi. But I still have Gabi in my life … every day if we want. I already miss her, and we've been apart for only three days. I feel sick thinking how hard it must be for Jeremy to live so far from his sister and Ethan. And being here—at my insistence—keeps reminding him of what he's missing.

I appreciate Jeremy and Laura's loyalty. Neither of them mentioned my drunken escapade to my mom. They pretend concern and sympathy when I say my oversleeping must be from jet lag. And when Mom insists on cooking us all Sunday brunch, and I blame my lack of appetite on something I ate last night, they back me up saying they thought the lamb looked a little greasy.

So things are going all right. I might survive this day. It's too much stress to even think about dinner with Jeremy's family tonight, but if I sit quietly … and maybe nap … I can make it through this afternoon.

Then, just after noon, Mom comes in from the patio and says, "It's a beautiful day. Is there a park we could we walk to?"

Ten minutes later, we step outside. A thousand needles pierce my eyeballs and my lids slam shut in self-defense. My fingernails digging into Jeremy's hand alerts him, and he pries his hand loose to guide me with an arm around my shoulders. How can I put the humiliation of last night out of my mind when I keep getting reminded?

"Bully," Jeremy whispers, not even trying to disguise his amusement.

And so it begins.

The park really is beautiful. It's Sunday, so a lot of people are around, but for the most part, they're quiet. We walk the paths and stop by the sculptured tulip beds just beginning to bloom. What a sight they'll be soon. We see herons and pea-cocks and, of course, pigeons and tons of other birds I don't recognize. Squirrels chitter and run around us. Jeremy says rabbits live in the park too, and sometimes pigs or cows are brought in to graze in the meadows, but we don't see any today.

My hangover has faded considerably. The fresh air and exercise are probably what I needed, and it makes me wonder if I didn't fool my mother at all with my fake complaints of jet lag and bad Indian food. She has a sixth sense about these things. Just as I know without him saying a word that Jeremy is stressing about dinner tonight.

I take his hand and lead him to a bench by the pond in the Japanese garden. My mom and Laura wander away, probably not by accident. "What will we have for dinner tonight, do you think?"

He sighs. "Something pretentious."

"Sounds delicious."

He squeezes my hand but doesn't smile. All his good humor from this morning has melted away. You'd think he was counting down the hours to his execution or something.

"Jeremy, what if your parents hate me?"

"I … why are you asking me that?" His back stiffens. He studies my face and then looks away toward the pond. "Are you saying you won't marry me unless they approve?"

Oh God. "Are you saying that?"

"Don't be absurd. Their opinion of you means nothing to me. Even less than nothing. Since they approved of Alison, their disapproval of you would be a point—ten points—in your favor."

"Then I should hope they dislike me?"

He sighs. "Please, just be yourself tonight."

He tips my face up to kiss me. I'm with the man I love, sitting in a beautiful garden, warmed by the sun, and soothed by the splashing of a waterfall. What could go wrong?

A peacock shrieks in my ear.

I jerk my head in the opposite direction that Jeremy turns his, causing a collision between my nose and his cheekbone, and yeah, thanks to my touchy nasal capillaries … nosebleed. It's all over both of us before he can find the pack of tissues in my purse.

The peacock shrieks again. It's stalking toward us. Ohmygod. I think they attack at the smell of blood.

"Run!"

By the time Jeremy catches up with me, I'm a good thirty yards away, approaching my mom and Laura who look horrified by my bloody hands and wad of tissues held to my face. He's laughing so hard he can barely breathe.

eight

The last time Jeremy smiled today was when he told Laura and Mom his version of "Chelsea and the killer peacock"—greatly exaggerated. At least that lightened his mood. For a while.

Now, we're driving to his parents' house, and he's glum and silent again. The knot in my stomach is so huge I doubt I'll be able to eat a bite, which will probably offend them … well, offend them more than just my presence in their home will. I don't see any way I can win this evening. But if I just keep my mouth shut—except for eating and drinking, of course—maybe I can make it through this dinner without further screwing up Jeremy's relationship with his family.

My mother smiles at me at the same instant Jeremy squeezes my hand. What? Are they twin mind readers now?

"Will I be meeting the daft prick tonight?" I ask him.

"The what?" For a second, Laura's eyes meet mine in the rearview mirror, then zip back to the traffic at the blare of a car horn.

"She means Richard," Jeremy tells her.

Laura frowns at me in the mirror.

"I'm just repeating what Jeremy calls him."

She glances back at Jeremy. "That's awful of you."

"Apt, though."

Laura laughs. "I have to admit it is."

"Oh, stop," my mom says, "I'm sure he's just as nice as his lovely siblings."

"As one of his siblings, thank you," Laura says, "but our brother Richard's been a spoiled brat since birth and shows no signs of outgrowing it."

Jeremy grumbles something to himself and then to me says, "Yes, you'll meet him tonight. Unfortunately."

Less than a minute later, Laura pulls up in front of a row of town houses. In the dark, I can tell only that the Pearce house is light-colored stone with at least three stories. I can't actually see the roof from inside the car, and the houses farther down the row have three or four floors so this one probably does too. Plus they all have those floors dropped below street level. But unlike the Notting Hill house, the Pearce home is fenced and gated and sits six steps up from the sidewalk, one amenity of living in this higher priced neighborhood, I guess.

Jeremy opens my door, and I get out. He's standing even straighter than usual like his whole body's clenched as tight as his jaw.

"We're still in London, right?"

"Chelsea," Laura says.

"Yes?"

Jeremy makes a breathy sound that might have been a "what?" I interpret it anyway from his arched brow. "I was responding to Laura."

"To me?" Laura frowns, looking from me to Jeremy and back. "I don't understand."

I'm just as confused. "You said my name."

Two seconds later, Laura says, "Ah." (Her grin is exactly like Jeremy's, only with lipstick—the perfect shade for her, by the way.) "You asked if we were still in London, and we are, but this district is Chelsea."

I smack Jeremy's arm. "Why didn't you tell me that?"

He shrugs—at least I think he does. He looks so tense it might have just been a nervous tic. Apparently, the cat's got not only his tongue, but his brain too.

"Well then"—my mother takes Jeremy's arm—"let's go inside."

"Right this way, Marie." Laura presses the car lock button on her key fob and moves toward the steps.

Reluctant though Jeremy is, he has no choice but to be dragged to the door by the mighty Marie Cole.

Laura opens the door to her parents' house, and we all file in. She and Jeremy take our coats and direct me and my mom to enter the room to the right off the entrance hall. Surely, they don't expect us to introduce ourselves to their parents. I glance at my mom. She smiles at me and squares her shoulders, obviously up to the challenge, and enters the room with me a step behind.

My first glimpse of the Pearce family home brings both admiration and disappointment. The entrance hall was impressive, and this living room, though surprisingly small, is beautiful too, gorgeously decorated and furnished in a classy contemporary style. I'm sure the house is totally worthy of an interiors magazine spread, but it's not the mansion I'd expected. I guess, in my mind, I'd exaggerated their wealth. Jeremy certainly hasn't given me any details. It occurs to me that maybe it wasn't his father's money he spent to live in California for six months to give writing a chance. Maybe it was Jeremy's whole future inheritance. I glance down at my left hand. Does this diamond ring represent the last of that? Is his fear that I'd discover his parents hadn't "disowned him," but that he'd already spent all they could give him the reason he didn't want me to meet them?

I won't discover anything about them just yet, though. This room is as empty of his parents as the hall was. It seems rude to me—and my mother, I'm sure—that Jeremy's parents haven't come out to greet us yet. Even if my mother is busy in the kitchen when company arrives at her house, she rushes out to welcome them. Mom and I are still standing when Laura and Jeremy enter.

"Please, make yourselves comfortable," Laura says.

Jeremy heads straight for the bar cart in the corner. He pours himself a double—at least—and downs it in two gulps.

"A G&T for me, brother dear." Laura turns to me and my mom. "And you'll have?"

"I'll have a gin and tonic too," Mom tells Jeremy as she settles on the sofa. "I've developed a taste for them."

I go to Jeremy and whisper, "Are your parents not here?"

He finishes making the drinks for Laura and my mom before he responds. "They're waiting upstairs in the drawing room. There's no tequila. How about a Batiste?"

"A what?"

"Rum and Grand Marnier."

I was really asking what he meant by drawing room, not that I've never heard the term; I've just never heard it come out of his mouth. I take the glass he's holding out. He serves the gin drinks and returns to the bar. I'm a little concerned when he pours himself another finger of Scotch.

"Drink up," he says to me. "You'll need it."

Seriously? My stomach clenches. If Jeremy and Laura both need drinks before they face their parents, how will I manage to get through this night?

After we've finished fortifying our courage, Laura leads us back into the hall and toward the stairs. As usual, Jeremy is the last to start the climb, but I'm determined not to enter the drawing room before him. I want him as a shield when I face the dragons.

As we near the open French doors, I hear them talking. They sound normal enough. A woman exclaims something. A man laughs. And then we're in the room—a much larger room than what I thought was the living room downstairs. Drawing room it is, with three huge windows in a bay, two sofas, and six armchairs, gleaming dark-wood flooring beneath three gorgeous area rugs, and over the fireplace hangs the largest mirror I've ever seen.

I feel so out of place. My mom looks totally at ease. Unlike me, she excels at always knowing how to fit in. I'm just always me—as unfortunate as that is sometimes.

While I've been taking the room in, I've avoided actually looking at the people. But now I have to because introductions have started. I assume the stately couple greeting my mom is Mr. and Mrs. Pearce. The other man in the room is handsome and looks a lot like Mr. Pearce, but though he looks a few years younger, his hair is grayer, so I'm sure that's not Richard. When the mystery man steps forward and gives Jeremy a smile and a hearty hug, I see how kind his eyes are.

Jeremy drops his guard and grins at him. "I didn't know you'd be here, Uncle Bert."

"What? And delay meeting your beautiful bride-to-be?" He smiles at me and holds out his hand. I prepare to shake it, but when he takes mine, he bows and kisses it.

I laugh. And then I want to smack myself. I look at Jeremy to see if he's as mortified as I feel, but he's still smiling. And so is his uncle.

"I'm sorry," I say. "I didn't mean to laugh. I just didn't expect … no one's ever kissed my hand like that before, but it was nice. I mean, you're nice. I was rude. Oh, crap. I'm screwing this up already, and I really didn't want—"

His uncle laughs. "You described her perfectly, son." He's still holding my hand, and now he squeezes it. "Chelsea, you are a pure delight." He pulls me into a hug and whispers, "Just don't expect hugs and kisses from the lord and lady."

The what and what?

He's joking, right?

Ohmygod.

Here they are, right in front of me. Jeremy's introducing me, but his words are muffled. I think I'm going to faint. They're smiling, but can I trust that? Crocodile smiles and all. Mine probably looks like the mouse's just before the cat eats it. I'm shaking hands. Seconds later, I'm invited to sit. Luckily, Jeremy guides me to one of the sofas and sort of pulls me down between him and my mother. What did I say to them? Did I say anything? Obviously nothing embarrassing or rude because everyone's still smiling. But that could just be politeness, right? I mean they're British.

I risk a glance at Jeremy. He's grim again, but then he's been grim all evening in anticipation of this meeting. Maybe I didn't humiliate him. I look at my mother. She's all smiles. And she's talking to Jeremy's mother. Lady Amanda Pearce!

Now that I'm not facing them, I take a closer look at Jeremy's parents. Lord Gordon might be about the same height as Jeremy, but he's built stockier and has coarser features. He looks so stern I can't imagine having to face him as judge.

It's Lady Amanda that Jeremy favors. I can't see the exact color of her eyes, but I think it's the same as his. And their noses have the same shape, though his is a bit longer. She looks feminine, and he doesn't, of course, but even more than the physical resemblance, they have the same … I don't know … an aura or something. You know they're intelligent and sensitive just by looking at them. But then, how could she be sensitive yet be so cold to her own son?

A woman appears in the doorway and announces dinner. They have a maid, housekeeper, whatever? Oh, of course they do. They're a lord and lady. I don't even know what those titles mean. Wait. Surely that was Uncle Bert's joke. Jeremy would have told me if his parents were royalty. Wouldn't he?

I'll kill him.

We move across the landing to the dining room. I take the chair Jeremy pulls out for me and sigh with relief when he sits next to me. I was afraid the lord and lady might separate us. I'm watching the maid serve the soup while trying to figure out if the kitchen of this house is on the same floor as the dining room or below it like at Laura's, so until Jeremy nudges me and looks toward his mother, I don't realize she's spoken to me.

"Sorry, could you repeat that?"

"I asked if you'd care to take tea with Laura, your mother, and me on Wednesday?"

"Yes, thank you." I'm not exactly sure what she means by "take tea," but I can't refuse, can I?

"Lovely," Lady Amanda says. "Claridge's at half past three, Laura?"

"Fine."

"Very well. I'll have Becky see to the reservation in the morning. We ladies will have a nice chat about the wedding."

Suddenly, the wedding Gabi and I have planned seems all wrong. I can't picture the lord and lady enjoying themselves in my mother's back yard. I take another spoonful of soup (what exactly is this?) confident that I'm doing it properly. I've picked up some proper dining etiquette from watching Jeremy eat, but I've never been able to manage the way he eats with his knife always in his right hand and his fork, tines down, in his left.

When the maid serves the next course, I thank her, and then I say, "How are you tonight?"

Her eyes practically pop out of her head. She shoots a look in Lady Amanda's direction—a look of alarm!—and then mutters a curt, "Fine, Miss," before moving on to serve Jeremy.

Ohmygod. I've clearly smashed to hell some social rule. My face is flaming. Jeremy pats my knee under the table. Did everyone hear? Light conversation seems to have continued, but I keep my eyes on my plate until I can breathe normally again. When I finally look up, Uncle Bert winks at me. It's a totally innocent wink. He's just trying to make me relax. I'm glad Jeremy has another ally in the family besides Laura. By the way, where's Richard?

As if I summoned him by thought, a man I assume is Richard walks into the dining room. He's shorter than Jeremy, actually closer to Laura's height. His hair is a blah light brown, but his eyes are a startling pale blue. Their color is the only thing that saves his face from being forgettable. He goes directly to his mother and kisses her cheek.

"Forgive me, Mummy. The traffic was absolutely dreadful." He sits next to her, making a show of settling his napkin on his lap. He doesn't even glance at Jeremy or me. "Father, I heard a rumor that one of the district judges has got himself in a fix with his bit on the side. Name?"

I can't take my eyes off him. Minus his rudeness, he's like a walking caricature of a prim and proper Brit. I glance across at Laura, and though her mouth is not smiling, her eyes are. She looks a question at me, which I interpret as—see?

Is it too late to cancel Richard's invitation to the wedding?

All in all, the rest of the dinner goes smoothly. The food is good, though I'm not sure what one of the side dishes is. I don't spill anything or commit anymore taboos ... as far as I know. As much as possible, I keep to my plan of silence. And though Lord Pearce speaks several times directly to Jeremy, I don't detect any particular animosity. I'm still confused why Jeremy dreaded this night so much—except for dealing with the daft prick, of course.

Richard monopolizes the conversation, which I imagine is the way it usually goes when he's around. I catch him looking at me a few times, but he never speaks to me. He does speak to Jeremy, updating him on people he'd known in the law office, which seems to interest only Richard. And as dessert is served, he asks Jeremy how the writing is going. The question sounds genuine, but Jeremy's curt response—"fine"—tells me Richard hadn't asked out of interest or concern but ridicule.

And then it's after nine o'clock, dinner is over, and we're up and moving back to the drawing room for coffee.

Coffee doesn't necessarily mean coffee, I see. Jeremy is already pouring himself a Scotch and Uncle Bert is taking drink orders. But Lady Amanda is pouring coffee in at least two of the cups set out on a tray, for herself and my mother, I presume, and I've just decided coffee would be the safest bet for me too, when Laura hands me a glass. Another Batiste. Before I can choose a place to sit, Richard is at my side, holding out his hand.

"I apologize for missing the formal introductions. I'm Richard, Jeremy's brother."

"Nice to meet you, Richard." He looks me up and down, pausing too long on my chest, and doesn't let go of my hand after we shake.

"It's obvious why Jeremy finds you so attractive."

He's rubbing his thumb along the back of my hand. I jerk it out of his.

He smirks. "I expect he could have had you at half the cost, though."

I try to push past him, but Richard has one more insult.

"Probably less." He moves aside.

Before I reach Jeremy, I see he's glaring at his brother.

"What did Richard say to you?" he asks.

"Nothing. He just introduced himself." I can tell by the way Jeremy looks at me he's not buying it, but he doesn't say anything more.

He leads me to the chair closest to one of the sofas—the one where his uncle is sitting beside my mother and beaming at her as she speaks. Jeremy sits, while I perch on the arm of the chair. While I'm sipping my drink and trying to keep up with three conversations at once, his fingers absently draw little circles on my lower back. Lord Gordon is standing by the fireplace discussing some law thing with Richard, Lady

Amanda is reminding Laura about participating in some festival, and Uncle Bert is flirting with my mom. Everyone's ignoring the two of us, and I'm pretty sure that's as fine with Jeremy as it is with me.

But then Lord Gordon sits down, and all conversation dies. He looks in our direction. "Jeremy, I encourage you to show Chelsea and Marie the best of our city this week. And then you'll join us in the country on Thursday."

Jeremy's hand falls away from my back. "For the whole weekend?"

"You'll be back here Monday afternoon. Is that too much to ask? I've arranged to take time off."

"We've already made plans in town with Laura."

His father holds out his empty glass to Richard, who jumps to refill it. "Surely, you haven't made plans that can't be postponed. And if, for a few hours, you need to come back to the city, you're welcome to use one of the cars. In any case, Laura will be staying with us too."

Laura's face shouts her surprise at that news.

For a moment, no one speaks.

"A family reunion," Uncle Bert cries. "I wouldn't miss it." He takes my mom's hand and then mine. "You ladies are in for a treat. The countryside should be bursting with the first of spring bloom."

"Likely, it will rain every day we're there," Richard says.

Lady Amanda sighs. "Don't grumble, dear."

I down the rest of my Batiste in one gulp.

Twenty minutes later, we're walking out to the car. Jeremy grabs the keys from Laura. She frowns at him but doesn't protest. He starts the car before I can get in beside him, and the second we've all shut our doors, he tears off down the street.

"Slow down," Laura tells him. "You're off your face."

"I assure you there's not enough alcohol in this fucking country—"

"Jeremy." He shoots a murderous look in my direction. I mouth, "My mom."

He winces and glances in the rearview mirror. "Sorry about that, Marie."

I'm just thankful there's not much traffic because he doesn't slow the car. He's still fuming.

"How could you neglect telling me what he had planned, Laura?"

"You think I knew?"

"Of course you knew."

"No, she didn't," I say. "I was watching her when your father told us his plans, and she was as surprised as you were."

"Thank you," Laura says.

"A weekend in the country sounds wonderful to me," Mom says.

No one responds.

She tries again. "Your uncle is very charming, Jeremy. He certainly seems fond of you."

Jeremy takes the corner a little slower. "Yes. He's a good man. And I love him too."

"He seemed to take quite an interest in you, Marie," Laura says.

"And you looked very happy with his interest, Mom."

"Oh," she says, flapping a hand dismissively, "he was just being hospitable."

When I look back, she's smiling to herself. Laura notices

too and says, "Uncle Bert is definitely preferable to Richard, wouldn't you say, Marie?"

"God, yes." My mother claps a hand over her mouth, and Laura and I laugh. Even Jeremy has to smile a little.

No one speaks during the last few blocks of the drive. I have so many questions to ask Jeremy, but I don't think he's in any mood to talk about his parents. Maybe Laura is. That plan is dashed a minute later when my mom yawns loudly, and Laura says she's exhausted too.

So the night ends with us all trooping straight up to bed.

And thanks to Lord Pearce, Jeremy doesn't even kiss me good night. He just gets in bed, turns away from me, and goes to sleep. Or pretends to.

I'm afraid I'll be awake all night, trying to figure out why this evening wasn't anything like I expected—well, except for Richard. I must be missing something. I kind of understand why Jeremy's angry that his father planned several days of our visit without consulting him, but since his parents paid for us to come here, I also kind of understand why they expected us to spend more time with them. His mom and dad weren't overly friendly to me, but they weren't rude either. And maybe they treated Jeremy a teeny bit coolish, but it didn't appear to me that they're "not the least bit interested" in him like he says. They certainly don't seem to hate him like he'd made me believe.

If this famous British reserve is strong enough that you can totally hide your true feelings, how does anyone here ever know what you really think of them?

nine

For the second time this week, I wake to find Jeremy's already up, and since he's not in the bedroom and the bathroom is dark, he's obviously already downstairs. After I brush my teeth and comb my hair, I get dressed and go down to the kitchen. Laura is sitting alone at the table, but Jeremy's visible through the patio door, pacing with his phone to his ear.

"Good morning," Laura says.

"Morning." I nod toward Jeremy. "What's up?"

"Ethan's commiserating with him about the change of plans."

I select my coffee and drop the K-Cup into the brewer. "My mom's not awake yet?"

"Oh yes, she's awake and already gone out."

I whip my head in Laura's direction. She's wearing an odd smile. "Gone out?"

"To breakfast with Uncle Bert."

"Wow. He didn't waste any time, did he?" I carry my cup to the table. "I like him."

"You should have seen the way Marie lit up when he called."

"Yeah?"

"Could it be love at first sight?"

"Believe me, my mom's way too practical for love at first sight." Suddenly I'm overcome with homesickness. "Would you remind me to call Gabi sometime this afternoon? The time difference keeps tripping me up. I sent her a photo of my dress, but we haven't had a chance to talk about it."

"Certainly."

"I wanted to ask Jeremy a question about your parents last night, but he wasn't in a talkative mood."

"Not surprising," she says. "Jeremy's a brooder."

"Well, he should have told me that your parents are a lord and lady."

"What? Where did you hear that?"

"Uncle Bert."

Laura's eyes are laughing, but she only smiles. "That's Uncle's way of criticizing them for their aspirations. My father is driven to become a high court judge. My mother's not driven, actually, just envious of a higher social status. So, no, they're not Lord and Lady Pearce."

"That's a relief."

"A relief?" She shakes her head. "Chelsea, you need to relax, or you'll crack spending a weekend around them." She bites her lip. "I don't know if I should tell you this, but the funny thing is that Uncle Bert, being the firstborn, is a lord, though it doesn't mean much today, and he wouldn't care if it did. The title originated long ago, when the family was wealthy and powerful."

I don't even want to imagine what Laura means by was wealthy. Is that the way all rich people think? I guess there's always someone with more money than you have. And I wish everyone would quit telling me to relax.

"I wonder if Uncle Bert told my mom he's a lord."

"I sincerely doubt that. Please don't mention it to her … or anyone."

I nod and finish my coffee. "What are we doing about breakfast?"

"Jeremy's call."

We both look toward the patio. He's pacing as he talks.

"Will it be so horrible for him to spend next weekend in the country? I mean, except for Richard, I thought it went pretty well last night."

Laura continues watching him. "The thing is … there's always a hostile undercurrent between Jeremy and our father. You can never predict when it will erupt. To Jeremy, Dad forcing him to spend several days in the same house with him is a subtle—or not so subtle—provocation."

"But why the hostility? I mean, I know your father disapproves of him giving up law."

"There is that."

"He says that neither of your parents care about him."

Laura gives me a wry smile. "I can't explain why he'd say that about Mum, but Dad?" She sighs. "Dad's not a flexible man. He truly loves the law and can't understand why Jeremy doesn't, especially since law has been the family business for generations."

"But what if you don't have the head for—"

"Ha! Jeremy's proficiency in the LPC is one reason Richard's so jealous of him."

"The LPC?"

"Legal practice course. It's a specialized training you take to qualify for a license to practice."

"Okay, I get that your father approves of Richard because he's chosen a law career, but you're an environmental conservationist, yet your relationship with him is not like Jeremy's, right?"

"But I'm a woman."

"Wow, so he's—"

"Sexist. Which explains a lot about Mum."

Jeremy's laughter rings out. Ethan's commiseration appears to have done the trick. He looks at me through the glass and smiles.

I smile back and stand. "I guess I'd better go get ready for the day."

Laura flips a hand toward the stairs. "Go."

♥ ♥ ♥

Uncle Bert has kept my mom occupied for most of the last two days. Yesterday, I saw her for about ten minutes in the morning and then had to wait up for her to get home so I could talk with her for twenty last night. Jeremy thinks it's nice that his uncle's been acting as my mother's tour guide. I guess I agree, partly because that's saved us from hours of suffering through the boring touristy stuff we're not interested in—and also the chore of remembering to censor ourselves in front of her. (Jeremy and Ethan get pretty foul when they're drinking together.)

Now, it's Wednesday afternoon, and Mom's way too excited about this tea thing with Amanda Pearce. I've asked Laura a million questions, so I know what to expect, and I'm not really looking forward to this experience. It doesn't sound like a good way to get to know my future mother-in-law. But I guess I'll have that chance this weekend.

Anyway.

I'm dressed appropriately in a cream cashmere sweater, camel wool slacks and jacket, and black pumps—nothing sexy at all. Jeremy comes upstairs as I'm putting on my shoes. He leans against the doorframe, arms crossed and staring at me.

"Those are not your clothes," he says.

"I told you I bought a few things."

"Did Gabi choose them for you?"

"Okay, yes. This is one of Gabi's work outfits. I borrowed some things from her." That confession earns me a disapproving scowl. "They're more appropriate."

He scoffs. "All you're missing is a pearl choker."

"I'm trying to fit in."

"Why would you want to look like … like … someone who's the opposite of you."

"Laura's not exactly the opposite of me."

"I wasn't referring to Laura."

"Then who?" I start transferring items from my usual bag to the designer clutch that goes with these shoes. When Jeremy doesn't answer, I look toward the door, but he's disappeared.

By the time I join Laura and my mom downstairs, Jeremy's left with Ethan. They're off to a pub, of course. The three of us leave for the hotel tearoom in a taxi to avoid parking problems. On the way, Mom points out places she's seen with Uncle Bert—Kensington Gardens, Hyde Park, Grosvenor Square Garden. It seems Uncle Bert has Mom figured out. They have another dinner date tonight.

From my Google search, I recognize the redbrick exterior of Claridge's, which only gives a hint of what's inside. The interior takes my breath away. Though I know it makes me look unsophisticated, I can't help turning in amazement to see all the views from the lobby. I have the oddest feeling I've been here before, and I was sad. Isn't that ridiculous?

"What do you think?" Laura asks.

"Gorgeous." My mom nudges my elbow. "Don't you think so, Chelsea?"

I close my gaping mouth and swallow back the lump in my throat. I still can't speak, so I nod.

Laura gestures toward a gorgeous staircase. "It's famous for its art deco style."

"Art deco," I whisper.

"Like your wedding dress," Mom says.

Laura glances toward the arches leading into the area where they serve tea. "Mum's rarely punctual, but she'll expect us to be seated and waiting."

"Oh, of course, let's go, Chelsea."

Mom tugs on my arm because I'm still gawking. Taking in every detail as we cross the black-and-white-tiled floor, I follow her and Laura. I'm a little keyed up, so I welcome the soft music playing. Gabi would love this place, and she would fit in just like my mom does. It's not like I'm deliberately clumsy, but, at the sight of all these white tablecloths, I feel doomed to spill tea, which I'm sure won't endear me to Jeremy's mother.

When we're seated, Laura informs the server that we're waiting for someone, and then she orders glasses of champagne for us. I hope she'll order the tea for me too because after one look at the selection menu online I was lost. The champagne arrives quickly. I'm thankful for that, and though I try not to sip too fast, I finish just as Amanda enters. It's not like me to be so nervous, but I need her to like me—or approve of me, at least—because that's the only hope I have of fixing things between Jeremy and his parents.

I've already learned Amanda's not big on hugging, so I'm not surprised when she simply greets us and takes her seat.

"We'll start with my usual," she says to the server. As he walks away, she looks to Mom. "Excuse me, Marie, I should have consulted you. Is oolong acceptable?"

"Perfectly, Amanda. Chelsea and I will be happy to follow your lead here."

Amanda smiles—at me too—and I relax a little. Laura winks at me. Is it so obvious I'm out of my element? A glance around the room reassures me that I look like I fit in. But the desire to be with Jeremy at the pub is overwhelming. Breathe, Chelsea, breathe.

"You've had such lovely weather for your visit," Amanda says, "but I'm afraid the forecast for this evening isn't as nice. What are your dinner plans, Laura?"

"I'm not sure for us yet. Marie will be with Uncle."

Amanda's eyes widen. "I hadn't heard, Marie. Albert's an excellent dinner companion."

"Yes, he is."

Amanda cocks her head and observes Mom with a slight smile, but she doesn't say anything more. I don't know Amanda well enough to read her smile. I give her the benefit of the doubt and assume it's not condescending or malicious. God, why would it be malicious? That's Jeremy's influence on my perception.

We're served delicious little sandwiches with the oolong, and then scones with a different tea. I'm trying to act like I've done this my whole life, so I lag behind Laura and Amanda a few seconds in all my movements. I glance up often to find Amanda watching me. Which means I'm looking at her more than I should be. Crap. I wish I could substitute more champagne for the tea.

So far, the conversation has been about our visit in London and the weather forecast for our country weekend, but now it turns to the wedding.

"Jeremy tells me you've decided on a garden wedding, Chelsea," Amanda says.

I lick a smudge of clotted cream from the corner of my mouth. "Yes. Our rose garden ... I mean Mom's garden. I don't grow roses. Or grow anything. Actually."

"A garden wedding sounds charming. And the date?"

"Um ... sometime in May. You're invited. I mean of course you are ... being Jeremy's parents ... obviously ..."

Laura bites back a smile.

Mom pats my hand.

Amanda arches her brows and looks to my mom. "Sometime?"

"They want an intimate wedding, Amanda, so elaborate planning hasn't been necessary, and since you and your family will be traveling the farthest, Chelsea wanted to consult you before setting the exact date."

I'm in awe of my mom. How does she come up with these things so quickly?

"Very well. I'll consult our schedules and let you know what's best for us when you come out to the country." Amanda gives me another smile I can't interpret. "What other wedding preparations have you made, Chelsea?"

"Well ... I have a dress."

"She bought it here, Mum," Laura says. "It's vintage. A lavender silk art deco style."

"Lovely."

"Made for Princess Grace of Monaco," my mom adds.

"Oh my."

"Jeremy likes it," I say, a little more defensively than I meant to. Well, no. I meant to defend the choice. I just didn't want it to sound like I was.

That smile again. "I can almost picture how beautiful you'll look, Chelsea."

Benefit of the doubt, Chelsea, benefit of the doubt. "Thanks."

We pause while the desserts are served. With another tea. No champagne.

When the servers leave, Amanda picks up the wedding talk again. "So, what sort of weather will you have in May?"

I stuff a bite of cake in my mouth. It's safer to let my mom and Laura do the talking.

"Perfect weather," Mom says. "It should be warm and sunny almost every day."

"Delightful. Gordon and I are—"

"Amanda?"

We all turn our heads toward the voice. Ohmygod. It's her. Alison. Jeremy's ex-sort-of-fiancée. As she leans down to air-kiss Amanda, Laura glares at her.

"Alison, why … my goodness." Amanda glances at me. "I … are you here with your mother?"

I search Amanda's face for evidence that she planned this meeting so she could show me the kind of woman she expected Jeremy to marry.

Alison laughs—musically, of course—and shows Amanda her left hand. Diamonds and emeralds glitter as she wiggles her fingers. "I'm here with my bridesmaids." She smirks at Laura.

"Oh, yes, we received the invitation last week," Amanda says.

"June weddings are so traditional, I know, but then traditions are honorable, don't you think? And mine will be the wedding of the season." She laughs again. "The entire year probably."

"No doubt," Laura deadpans.

Amanda flashes a look at Laura and then gestures toward my mom. "Alison, this is Marie Cole."

"Good afternoon," Alison says, obviously not happy at having her wedding gush interrupted.

"And you've already met her daughter," Laura says.

Alison looks at me with not a hint of recognition. "I don't believe so."

"Chelsea Cole," Laura adds, "you met her in California. Outside Jeremy's flat."

Alison's face hardens as fast as a drop of melted wax hitting an ice cube. Laura grabs my left hand and lifts it to show Alison my ring.

"They're getting married … in May."

"Congratulations," Alison says through gritted teeth and a rictus smile. She turns back to Amanda. "It was nice to see you, Amanda."

We watch as Alison stalks toward a group of women standing on the far side of the lobby. I look away first and back at Amanda. Was her glance at Laura out of fear her daughter might mess up her plan to humiliate me? I'm still wondering when Amanda turns to me.

"I'm sorry that happened, Chelsea."

Before I can respond, she grins. Then a giggle bubbles out, and she presses her napkin to her mouth as if to prevent another one escaping.

"But," she adds, her eyes sparkling, "isn't it fortunate that you planned your wedding for May?"

We're all smiling as we return to our desserts and tea. I'm relieved but confused. Jeremy led me to believe his mother had practically arranged his marriage to Alison, so what's changed? If she approved of Alison so much, how could she accept me as a replacement?

A few minutes later, I realize that Alison and I were dressed almost identically. Except for her pearl choker.

A chorus of happy men's voices ring out when Laura answers her door. A few seconds later, a crowd of six men burst into the living room with Ethan at the head.

"We're kidnapping Jeremy," he announces. "Impromptu stag night."

"But"—Jeremy looks to me—"our dinner plans ..."

He's struggling to hold back a grin.

"No big deal," I say, "we have dinner every night. Go on."

"Thanks." He kisses me quickly, and the man pack files back out past Laura.

"Well," she says, "it's just you and me tonight."

I'm too preoccupied with a sudden bad feeling about this stag night business to do more than nod.

"Something wrong? You aren't angry about Jeremy going —"

"No. Of course not. And it will be fun, just the two of us."

"It will, so let's change plans. We'll have a quick dinner and then make the rounds of some of my fave spots for drinks."

"A girls' night out."

Laura looks down at her outfit—a cashmere sweater and wool slacks. "But first we need to glam it up a bit."

"Sure."

We head to our rooms to change. I don't know what Laura considers glam, but it's probably not what I'm thinking, so it's a good thing I didn't bring any of my regular party outfits. After seeing how Alison was dressed today, I changed clothes the minute we got home. So I keep on my skinny jeans, but trade my wool cowl-neck sweater for a white silky V-neck one and my boots for red stilettos. Still pretty conservative but dressier. I spice up my eye makeup and head to Laura's room.

Her door is open. I don't see her, but when I step into the room, I hear her moving around in the bathroom. "Laura?"

"Almost ready."

A moment later, she steps out. Totally transformed. Her hair is pulled up in a messy topknot, leaving several loose tendrils that look effortlessly artful. She's wearing a black bodycon mini dress with spike-heeled ankle boots. And then she totally rocks it by slipping on a purple leather bolero jacket.

By comparison, I look like a middle-aged mom. The look she gives me agrees.

"Chelsea? What the hell!"

"Pretty lame, huh?"

"Definitely not the bomb ass you I met in California."

"I wanted to make a good impression. On your parents."

"Well, we won't be seeing them tonight." She beckons me to follow her into her closet. "We're the same size, I think."

Ten minutes later, dressed in a black bustier skater dress, I feel like myself for the first time since we arrived in London.

"Perfect," she says. "And I have a killer red jacket that will match your shoes, but first … your hair. I don't have any color spray, but we can spike it up or do something to make it more your style."

Twenty minutes later, we're eating fish and chips from a nearby shop. Laura assures me the grease coating our stomachs will allow us to drink more without getting "pissed." The taxi drops us at a club called Sync, where we drink lavender martinis and dance. We leave with Becky, a friend of Laura's, in tow. At the second club, Bling, their friend Prisha joins us and we drink Ginger Balls. Men try to join our group too, but though we dance with them, they're not invited to sit with us. After a while, the four of us take "the tube" to a third club. I don't catch this one's name. Apparently, the second Ginger Balls burned off the grease coating my stomach. We're all laughing a lot and too loudly, but we're girls on a night out, so we order Cosmopolitans.

I'm done with dancing after just one Cosmo and decline the third round. I'm homesick for Gabi, and tears sting my eyes when I wonder what Jeremy's doing right now, so I don't argue when Laura calls it a night explaining that we have morning plans before we're off to the country. Because Becky and Prisha aren't ready to leave, we all hug and part ways.

Outside, too woozy to decide whether to call a taxi or take the tube back to Laura's, we just start walking. I feel surprisingly warm. Suddenly I remember the first night Jeremy and I got high together, and tears spill over my lashes. "I love him so much."

"I hope you're talking about my brother."

"Jeremy's wonderful and sweet and smart and … and … great. He's just great. Don't you think he's great, Laura?"

Teared up herself, she just nods.

"We're drunk, aren't we?"

She nods again. A minute later she says, "It's raining."

It is. We're already half soaked. She grabs my arm, and we stumble into the pub across the street. It's loud and crowded.

"Find us a table," she says. "I'm going to the loo."

I don't see any empty tables, but then everything's a little blurry. I might be swaying a teeny, tiny, little bit. I grab onto a post by the door and squint, concentrating harder. A burst of laughter draws my attention to a group in one corner. The jolly bunch is several guys and one … two … three women. Ohmygod. I stop breathing. The woman at the center of the group is sitting next to Jeremy. Fuck that. Let's tell it like it is —the bitch is practically sitting on his lap. And worse—yes, it gets worse—for the second time today, I'm looking at that slut Alison.

"Chelsea, why are you still stand—"

Yep. I'm not hallucinating. Laura sees them too.

"It's not what you think," she says, starting toward them.

I grab her arm. "Don't."

"Why not?"

I shake my head and stumble back outside. Laura catches up with me a half block from the pub.

"Let's go back in and see what's—"

"Why would Ethan do that? I thought he liked me."

"He does. Ethan didn't invite her to join them. I'm sure of that."

It's still raining. Laura pulls me under an awning and calls for a taxi. Then she dials again.

"Who are you calling?"

She gives me the one-finger-wait-a-sec sign. "Ethan? It's Laura. Take this call outside."

I'm furious and try to grab her phone, but she turns her back and holds me off.

"I'm with Chelsea," she says. "We're down the street. Look to your right." She waves at him, and he jogs our way.

"Why are you two out here in the rain?"

"We were just in the pub," she tells him.

"Yeah? Why didn't you—" His eyes widen. "Oh."

"Explain."

He holds up both hands palms forward. "They pushed their way into our group. I swear. No one invited them." He turns to me. "Jeremy has no blame in this."

"Bullshit," I say. "He seemed pretty cozy with Alison a few minutes ago."

"That's all her. I swear it. If he was sober, he would have none of that."

Laura grabs his shoulder and turns him back to her. "You seem sober enough to take care of it for him, Ethan."

"Too right. I'll do that. I should have done. I'll do it now. Statim."

She points a finger at him. "Do not tell Jeremy that Chelsea saw him." Ethan nods. "I'm serious about that, Ethan. You know I will make your life miserable if you tell him."

He raises his right hand. "Not a word." Laura gives him a push toward the pub. He takes an unsteady step or two, and then lowers his head and rushes forward to get out of the rain.

"Do you believe that Jeremy is innocent?" Laura asks.

"Come on, Laura. How could he be so drunk he doesn't realize she's hanging all over him?"

"I take it you've never seen him completely shit-faced."

I open my mouth to protest. But she's right. I've seen Jeremy high or with a buzz, but never really, really drunk. "I hate that bitch. I'd like to rip her hair out."

The taxi pulls up to the curb.

"As much as I'd love to see that, we'd best go home."

We ride for a few minutes in silence before I question

Laura. "Why did you tell Ethan not to let Jeremy know we saw him?"

"I didn't want Alison to have that satisfaction."

I link arms with her and lean my head on her shoulder. Isn't it great to have a future sister-in-law who's got your back … especially when she lets you borrow her clothes?

"And," she says, "we don't want to give him time to make up a lie."

ten

For the first few seconds after I wake, I lie with my eyes closed, thinking I'm at home. Then last night flashes before me, and I sit up. Jeremy's not in bed. There's not even a dent in his pillow where his head should have been. Just to be sure, I scramble to the foot of the bed and then his side looking for his clothes on the floor. Nothing there or on any of the chairs in the room. I might have slept through his coming in last night, but there's no way he got up this morning, showered, and dressed without waking me.

I picture him with Alison, and my stomach flips. I'm certain I'm about to vomit, when another possibility surfaces. Ethan. Thank you, God. Ethan must have taken Jeremy home with him. I throw on a shirt and jeans and head for the stairs.

The smell of coffee pulls me all the way down to the kitchen. Laura and my mom are sitting at the table. I hold up my phone. "Can you give me Ethan's number?" I ask Laura.

"Why?"

"Jeremy must be there. He didn't come home last night."

"Yes, he did," my mom says.

"He made it as far as the sofa," Laura adds. "That's probably a good thing. He might have broken his neck if he'd tried to climb the stairs."

I run back up a flight to the living room. Jeremy is sprawled facedown on the sofa, still dressed in last night's clothes … or most of them. His socks and shoes are nowhere in sight. I kick him in the knee. "Get up!"

He shoots to his feet. Then he clutches his head and collapses back on the sofa with a groan. I go back down to the kitchen and make two cups of coffee. When I return to the living room, he's lying down again.

"Sit up and drink this."

He gives me a slightly unfocused glare but sits up and takes the cup.

"How was your stag night?"

"Drank too much."

"With the guys?"

His nod is followed by another groan. I wait, sipping my coffee while he drinks half of his.

"So. Just you and the guys, huh?"

His brow creases. His eyes shift back and forth as he replays the night. I can tell the exact second he remembers Alison by the way his brow clears and he sits upright. He swallows. He doesn't look at me.

"If you're trying to think up a lie, don't bother. I was there."

Now he looks at me, frowning deeper than before. "You were there? I don't remember—"

"You didn't see me. I didn't hang around when I saw that bitch draped all over you."

"She wasn't. At least … I don't think she was." He heaves a sigh. "I was completely pissed, Chelsea."

"So then you don't really have any idea what you did or didn't do."

"I wouldn't do—" He sits up straighter. "We spent the whole night in pubs. I'm sure of that. So I couldn't have—"

"Have you forgotten that night we were in the women's restroom at—"

"I didn't do that or anything close to it last night."

"Except you were 'completely pissed,' so …"

He slumps forward, holding his head. I wait.

After a couple of minutes, he gets to his feet slowly. "I have witnesses. Ask Ethan"—he pulls his phone from his pocket and holds it out to me—"and my other mates' numbers are in there too. Call them all." He shakes his phone at me. "Take it. They will also tell you I had no idea she or any women would join us and that I did not cheat on you in any way."

"Put your phone away. Ethan already cleared you."

"When?"

"Last night. Laura called him out of the pub after we saw you."

He sits back down. With elbows resting on his knees, he focuses on his clasped hands. "I'm sorry you saw me like that."

"I'll bet you are."

"I meant the drinking. But I'm also sorry for whatever else you saw, which wouldn't have happened if I'd been sober."

"Wouldn't have been much of a stag night if you'd been sober."

He looks up at me. I smile. He sighs.

"I really do love you," he says.

"You'd damn well better, dude. Now get in the shower. You probably stink of her perfume."

♥

Twenty minutes later, Jeremy joins us in the kitchen. He chooses his coffee and starts it brewing.

"The forecast is for sun all day," Laura says. "I thought we'd go up to Camden Market. One last hurrah before we head to the country."

"Mm-hmm." Jeremy leans back against the counter sipping his coffee.

"Oh, Jemmy, let's see if we can get a transport on the canal."

"Why?"

"But first, let's walk over to Tabernacle for breakfast. Couldn't you murder a nice plate of juicy sausage and runny eggs before the boat ride, Jemmy?"

Queasiness washes over Jeremy's face.

"Bad deal if the water's rough, though," Laura says. "You know how it is when a boat's bobbing up and down and up and down and—"

Jeremy groans. "You are the devil's spawn, Lolly."

Laura grins.

"I'll bet life would have been fun growing up with you two," I say.

"You didn't torment your brothers, Chelsea?"

"No," I say at the same time my mother says the opposite.

"You most certainly did," she says.

"And then you would tell your father they'd started it," Jeremy says.

"You weren't there."

"Ah, but I've spoken to your brothers."

"Well, they deserved it," I say.

"You lied to get Scott and Ryan in trouble?" my mom says, offended. "And I took your side."

I shoot Jeremy a deadly look. "They picked on me at other times, Mom."

"Precisely," Laura says. "You take your revenge when you can."

We fist-bump.

My mom and Jeremy are shaking their heads in reproof at both of us.

Laura stands. "Let's get ready, ladies. Enjoy your coffee and quiet while it lasts, brother."

We leave him in the kitchen and go upstairs. After a quick shower, I blow-dry my hair. It's still a shock to see myself in the mirror. I haven't had hair this dull since I was eleven—no, even that summer, Gabi and I experimented by dying our hair with Kool-Aid. It didn't show much on her dark hair, but I had some pretty wild colors going until my mom put her foot down. Oh, well, boring hair is a small sacrifice to help ease things with the lord and lady.

Jeremy's here when I come out of the bathroom. He's standing by his old desk, looking out the window.

"I did our laundry," I say.

He nods but doesn't look at me.

"Have you packed yet?"

"Yes."

"I just have a few things left to pack when we get back this afternoon." He says nothing, so I go to stand beside him, but he pulls me in front and wraps his arms around me.

"What did you think of my parent's town house?"

"It's beautiful. I've never seen a drawing room ... well, on TV, but I've never actually been in a room like that. It made me feel elegant. And this house is gorgeous too. How could you stand living at Ocean View?"

He stiffens and drops his arms to his sides but says nothing. I feel stupid just standing in front of him, so I turn, look up, and smile, which is no less awkward because he's looking over my head, still staring out the window. I'm not sure what's up, but I'm probably better off letting him work it out on his own. I leave him at the window and put on my wool coat and scarf and hat, tucking my gloves into a pocket. (I don't trust the sun here anymore.)

As I watch him gazing out at the city he loves, I mentally slap myself for being so dense. Why do I keep saying things that remind him of what he would still have if he'd never moved to California?

After another minute, I say, "I guess we'd better go."

Without a word, Jeremy grabs his jacket and heads for the stairs.

If I thought Jeremy was glum leading up to the dinner with his parents the other night, that's nothing compared to the state he's in by the time we get in Ethan's car to drive to the country house. Laura and my mom, who are driving there separately because we have too much luggage to fit along with the four of us in her car, left a few minutes before us because Jeremy was stalling.

As we head out, Ethan prods Jeremy to cheer up. "Come on, mate, you're not headed to your execution."

Jeremy scoffs. "No, that would be over quickly."

"It's only a weekend."

"Four days. In hell."

Ethan's golden gaze seeks my eyes through the rearview mirror, signaling that he tried.

I take his cue. "We don't have to spend the whole time there. Your father said we could take a car to London anytime."

Jeremy turns in his seat to look at me. "At best, that's an hour's drive. One way."

"Well, then I guess we'll just have to hide in our room a lot … having sex."

Ethan laughs and pumps a fist in the air. "My kind of girl."

Jeremy growls and goes back to staring out his window.

Crap. If no one speaks, an hour's drive will take forever. "Why don't you stay too, Ethan?"

He meets my eyes in the mirror again. "Gordon views me as a bad influence on his son."

"But you're a lawyer."

"Yes, but I failed to dissuade Jeremy from his 'fool's errand' of pursuing novel writing. No, not failed. I didn't try."

"I'm sorry you're not welcome there."

"He was never fond of me anyway. I seemed to always be involved whenever our Jeremy got himself in a spot of trouble." Ethan's grinning. He elbows Jeremy. "Remember the time we nicked your dad's Austin and got it mired in the bog?"

Jeremy barely grunts.

"We were thirteen," Ethan tells me. "And how about the time I talked you into gifting Sheila a pair of your mum's diamond earrings?" Again, he adds for my benefit, "Convinced him she had so many she'd never miss them. Turns out she was particularly fond of that pair and noticed immediately. And, naturally, they were a bit pricey."

"How old were you then?" I ask.

"Fifteen."

"Fortunately, Sheila's parents made her give them back before Jeremy had to ask for them."

Jeremy huffs and shakes his head.

"This is comforting," I say. Ethan's eyes ask for an explanation. "I'm glad to know he wasn't always perfect."

Jeremy and Ethan exchange a look. But then Ethan's laughter sends Jeremy back to his window. After that, we ride mostly with only the radio breaking the silence.

And then we arrive.

You know that feeling where, for just a second, you can't believe what you're seeing is real? That happens to me as we enter the driveway through huge iron gates—Dovewood House reads the plaque on one of the gate pillars. Enhanced by the first glow of sunset, the view of the Pearce country house reminds me of a scene in one of those movies Gabi and I love ... the ones made from Jane Austen books. Not that Dovewood House is a match for the colossal mansion Mr. Darcy lived in, but it's big and old and ... well, grand. A manor house.

I glance at Jeremy and discover that he's been watching me. Watching my reaction. I close my gaping mouth and smile. "Impressive."

He says nothing and faces forward again. Laura and my mom, who beat us here, are standing outside their car. A man I don't recognize is helping them unload the luggage ... the butler, I suppose. Probably one of many servants, considering the size of this house. Jeremy grew up here. This was his life. Now, I better understand Alison's reaction—"you've got to be kidding"—when she saw the apartments where Jeremy and I lived.

It's hard not to feel like a girl from the wrong side of the tracks, snooping to see how the other half lives. I can't wait to have a few minutes alone to send Gabi some photos.

Jeremy opens my door and helps me out. "It's just a house," he mutters.

Ethan empties his trunk of our suitcases. "Ring me when you're going to be in the city," he says and moves to get back in the car.

Jeremy grabs his arm. "Where do you think you're going?" Ethan flicks his eyes toward the house. Jeremy shakes his head. "If I can abide him for a weekend, you can for a few hours."

Ethan picks up two of the bags he'd just sat down. "You owe me."

Jeremy grabs the other suitcase. Taking me by the hand, he leads our group into the house though a heavy arched door.

He and Ethan set the luggage on the gleaming wide-planked floor where the butler is standing with the rest. As we move farther into the house, I try my hardest not to gasp or gawk or react in any way other than casual curiosity, but it's almost impossible.

The entry hall, surely thirty feet long and ten wide, leads to a room that's at least as large as my mother's living room and seems to be only a wider hall. In the center, a beautiful round pedestal table with a huge floral centerpiece sits under a massive chandelier and a few occasional chairs are set against the wall between doors opening onto other rooms. One surprise is that to my right an indoor pool is visible through French doors. Another surprise is that it's brighter in the hall and whatever this room is than I expected, but I have a feeling the walls and woodwork now painted cream and white used to be much darker when the house was built.

"When was this house built?" Mom asks.

"Oh, not so long ago," Laura says, "1836, I think."

I'm still trying to grasp that in England nearly two centuries is "not so long ago" when Amanda appears in an open doorway across the room.

"Welcome to Dovewood House," she says. "The Pearce family has held title to the land for over three centuries, and the original manor house, built in 1798, was replaced with this one, which has been enlarged twice and remodeled three times that I know of. Paintings of both original houses are hanging in the drawing room if you're interested." She sweeps an arm toward the room she just left. "Come join me for tea." She winks at Ethan. "Gordon hasn't arrived yet, but we won't let that stop us."

We enter another white room. Although the architectural detail is the same as the two halls, the furnishings are more casual, more modern, but no doubt expensive. I scan the walls for the paintings Amanda told us about, but evidently this is not the drawing room. The arrangement of the sofas and chairs at this end of the room frustrates me because on the wall at the far end, beyond the piano, hangs an assortment of what looks like black-and-white family photos. I can't wait to get close enough to study them.

Amanda gestures for us to sit. "Please make yourself comfortable. Jeremy, will you see to the drinks?"

He glances at Mom as he moves toward the bar. "G&T, Marie?"

"Yes, thank you, dear."

Either knowing or assuming, Jeremy doesn't ask for anyone else's order.

"Shall we?" Amanda says, gesturing to the display of food on the tea cart being wheeled in by a servant. "I hope you enjoyed the drive. It's lovely countryside here, though not as breathtaking as it will be in a couple of weeks when all the trees have leafed out and flowers are blooming everywhere."

"But, Amanda," Mom says, "it's still a gorgeous land-scape."

We're silent for a few minutes, nibbling and drinking. With plates being passed around and balanced on our knees, it's all more casual than the tea at Claridge's, but with my tendency to clumsiness, it's still stressful.

"Uncle hasn't arrived yet?" Laura asks.

"Oh yes. He spent most of the afternoon riding, so he's probably in the stable now."

Mom perks up. "You have horses?"

I'm surprised at her reaction until I remember she was raised on a farm. I never saw it because her parents died years before I was born. She inherited the place but had to sell it to pay off their debts. By then, she'd already moved to the city and met my father, so I didn't think she regretted letting the farm go, but maybe I was wrong.

"They're Bert's pride and joy," Amanda tells my mom. "He's always been a horse lover. Do you ride?"

"I used to."

Amanda smiles. "Then I expect you will again this week-end." She turns to Ethan. "How is your mother?"

"Off on another honeymoon, so I expect she's happy ... for now."

Amanda pauses only a second. "And your father?"

"He's retiring next month. Says he's moving out of the country."

Jeremy's face registers surprise. "Where to?"

Ethan shrugs. "I give him a month before he's working again. Retirement is a foreign concept to him."

Amanda sighs. "I think it's the generation. I can't imagine Gordon ever retiring."

"They're defined by their occupations, Mum," Laura says.

The room is quiet for a moment again before Uncle Bert enters.

"Halloo! Why is everyone so glum on this fine afternoon?"

Mom beams at him.

Jeremy smiles and moves back to the bar. "The usual, Uncle?"

"Brilliant. Thank you, dear boy."

I'm wondering where Richard is, but since no one's mentioned him, I won't either. It would suit some of us, at least, if he stays in town this weekend. He's an agitator, so his absence might even keep things civil between Jeremy and his father.

"The forecast calls for clear skies again tomorrow." Uncle Bert accepts his drink from Jeremy and then takes a seat beside Mom. "I do believe you've brought the sun with you, Marie." He pats her hand and then leaves his over hers.

I glance at Jeremy who nods toward them and then raises his eyebrows. I shrug. I really need to get some time alone with Mom to find out what's going on there. It feels strange to see her with a man and glowing like that.

The conversation roams from topic to topic, all pleasant, until, during a moment's lull, Gordon's angry voice carries to us, growing louder as he nears.

"Take care of it," he growls and enters the room, pocketing his phone. Richard, who enters on his father's heels, goes straight to the bar to pour the man a drink. "Forgive me," Gordon says, nodding to Mom and me. "I thought I'd left work at the office." He takes the glass from Richard without a thank-you or even a glance. "Has Amanda given you the house tour yet?"

"I waited for you," Amanda says. "We'll go after we finish tea."

"Very well." Sighing, he sits.

Richard's at the bar pouring himself another drink when Gordon announces it's time for the tour.

"Would anyone else care to refresh their drink before we go?" Amanda asks.

Jeremy and Ethan pour doubles for themselves.

"I'll wait here," Richard says, and I almost feel sorry for him when no one tries to convince him to come along.

Although I'm curious as hell to see every inch of this house, it's evident from the start that Jeremy's irritated by his father's insistence on conducting a tour. It does seem snooty to me for a moment, but then I think about the family owning this property for centuries and decide that gives Gordon a right to be proud. As he leads the way, Jeremy and Ethan hang back muttering rude comments under their breath, which seems childish to me, so I move up beside Laura.

Gordon shows us his study, the library, and the dining room, which are all paneled in dark wood like I expected the whole house to be. But the walls of Amanda's sitting room are covered in elegant wallpaper in a rose shade. The sofa and chairs are upholstered in pastel or floral fabrics. And a grace-ful white desk sits in front of one window. We pass a closed door on the left and a wide staircase to the right as Gordon leads us to what he calls the reception hall. (Turns out this is the big room with the round table under the chandelier.) He opens the French doors leading to the pool, and we file in to stand on the stone deck as he points out the "solarium" on the far side and the changing room to our right. Another set of French doors, at one end of the pool, lead outside.

"Amanda and Jeremy are so fond of swimming that we remodeled to convert the old ballroom into our indoor pool area," he says. "You'll see the outdoor pool tomorrow."

Two pools!

"You said the old ballroom?" my mom says.

Amanda nods. "We have a new one in the new wing."

A ballroom!

The new wing!

Gordon leads us through the last door opening off the reception hall. The same gleaming, wide-plank flooring extends throughout this floor, covered with beautiful area carpets, some oriental, some solid-colored plush or Berber. A beautiful dark red oriental covers the center of this room, which is also paneled. A massive painting hangs above an equally impressive fireplace.

"Dovewood House as it looked soon after its major renovation," Gordon announces with a gesture toward the painting. "And there"—he points to the opposite wall—"is a depiction of the original manor house."

The original was only two floors and white stone, not tan brick like this one, but both paintings show the same beautiful green landscape with several detached buildings of various sizes.

"All the rooms I've shown you and the ones directly above are part of the original house. Obviously, many of the rooms have been remodeled. Amanda demanded larger windows for more natural light. The coach house and new wing are now connected by a hall extending past the original cloakroom. Follow me."

Cloakroom!

I'm a little disappointed when he turns in the opposite direction from the beautiful staircase we passed earlier. He leads us back toward the front entrance but turns left into a narrower hallway before we reach that door. I'd barely registered that our luggage had been left by this hall. It's gone now, of course, carried up to our rooms by the butler I suppose.

(I feel ridiculous even thinking about servants.)

We pass closed doors and a narrow stairway without any comment from Gordon, but Laura and I have lagged back enough that we're in range of Jeremy's sarcastic whisper. "To our left, we have the dark passage leading to our servant quarters."

Ethan snickers.

Laura turns her head slightly toward them and whispers, "Our staff quarters, Jeremy. Don't provoke Dad."

"Watch out," Ethan whispers. "Chelsea's about to call you a bully."

Laura slaps a hand over her mouth to hide her grin.

I take a giant step forward. I don't know why the three of them didn't stay behind. It's not like they've never seen this house before.

Gordon points out the almost elegant four-car garage, then shows us the totally modern media room and then the ballroom, which is mostly just a huge, empty room with massive mirrors the length of one long wall and, along the opposite wall, more of those floor-to-ceiling windows and two sets of French doors that open out onto a patio. A grand piano sits in one corner with a few wooden chairs nearby. It's everything a ballroom should be, I guess, if you're the type of person who holds balls. Above the ballroom are a game room and a fitness room with all the professional exercise equipment you could want. Seriously.

Mom, of course, has been saying all the appropriate things. I'm sort of freaked out, so I mostly smile and keep quiet. There's rich, and then there's rich. Jeremy's family is rich, and that's not what I was prepared for. Why is he living in California, in Mom's middle-class suburban ranch house, when he could have all this?

I'm stunned. Not counting the pool area and staff rooms, I've now seen, or been told exist, twenty-some rooms. Literally, I lost count. I'm seeing Jeremy in a whole new light. Well, actually, I'm seeing him in two new lights. Even though he comes from a social class higher than I dreamed, he's acting a lot less stuffy than he does back home. Kind of immature really. Partly, that's the effect Ethan has on him, and I sort of understand that, but I'm surprised that even Jeremy is having trouble adulting in his childhood home.

On the pretense of "getting some air," Jeremy, Ethan, Laura, and I are standing behind the house on part of a huge patio, which they call a terrace. We're passing around an enormous spliff, as Ethan called it when he pulled it out of his jacket pocket. Actually, I took only one hit because it's primo shit, and I don't trust myself to make it safely through dinner if I'm high. Which is too bad. I could use something to mellow out after Jeremy and Ethan's behavior during the house tour. And there Jeremy goes again, mocking his father.

"To my left, you'll see another ostentatious display of my wealth," Jeremy says, "a genuine Grecian urn planted with a rare species I personally saved from extinction."

Okay. That's enough. "You're acting like a child, Jeremy."

It seems to take a second for my words to reach him, and then he straightens to his Mr. High Tea posture. "You know how my—"

"Yeah, yeah, I know. You have a big, mean daddy. But you're a man now, not a ten-year-old, so grow a pair."

He couldn't look more incredulous. His face reddens, and he starts to sputter—honest to God. Just when I fear he's going to blow, Ethan punches him in the shoulder. The blow knocks Jeremy back a foot or two, but he keeps his balance. The three of us watch him. He's not moving, just staring ahead.

And then he starts laughing.

Ethan points at Jeremy. "You'd better appreciate what you've got in this woman, arsehole."

Jeremy reins in his laughter. "I do, mate. I do." He reaches out and pulls me to him for a kiss. "I'll do my best to act the man."

"Won't be easy with him around." Giggling, Laura gestures toward Ethan. "Away, you three-inch fool!"

"Hide not thy poison with such sugared words," he replies.

Jeremy snaps to attention and proclaims, "More of your conversation would infect my brain." He bows. "I will be bold and take my leave of you."

The three of them nearly fall over roaring with laughter. I just walk away shaking my head. Looks like I might not be the one in danger of making a disaster of dinner after all.

Mom meets me at the door. "I was just coming to tell you we're going in to dinner." She waves in the Shakespearean comedy troupe behind me.

Gordon and Amanda insisted that Ethan stay, which makes us nine at the table. Just as I'm about to take the chair Jeremy's pulled out for me, Gordon speaks.

"Please, Marie and Chelsea, sit by me. Amanda had you for tea, but I've not had much chance to enjoy your company."

Amanda and Gordon take their usual places at opposite ends of the table while the rest of us shuffle around. Mom and I move to each side of Gordon. But Amanda stops Jeremy from sitting next to me.

"Here please, Jeremy." Amanda indicates the chair to her right. Richard, frowning because he'd been about to sit there, instead claims the chair to her left.

Uncle Bert sits beside Mom, and Ethan moves to Jeremy's side, leaving Laura to choose either the chair between me and Ethan or Richard and Uncle Bert. I beckon her with my eyes and am relieved when she comes to my side. Game of Thrones pops into my mind because it feels like we're positioning for battle.

This time, I know not to try to chat with the "staff." But I'll have to speak to Gordon, obviously, unless my mother monopolizes his attention. Please do, Mom. I'd rather listen and learn.

"Chelsea," Gordon says before I've had a single taste of the soup, "what do you think of our England?"

"I love it. Even if it is cold."

"You find us unwelcoming?"

"Oh. No. I meant the weather. I was already prepared for the people to be reserved. Like Jeremy."

Gordon glances down the table toward Jeremy. "Is he?"

"Well, he's not as snooty as he used to be. And I guess I

partly got the wrong impression of that. He was really just kind of shy around me."

Gordon's eyebrows shoot upward. "Shy?"

"Yeah. But still, he can be stuffy. Maybe not what you—"

"Albert has shown me so many fascinating places in London," my mom says.

For a moment, Gordon seems perplexed at Mom's deflection. Then he smiles at her and looks quizzically at Albert. I guess he hadn't heard they'd been dating … if that's what it is they're doing. I take advantage of Gordon's attention being on my mom telling him about all those fascinating places to tune into the conversation at the other end of the table.

"… that those plans are already finalized," Jeremy tells his mother.

"I did. But you know your father. He's already decided to make the offer."

"Could you ask him not to, please?"

"I would think you'd be grateful, Jeremy," Richard says. "Your wedding should be an event in this community."

Our wedding? They're discussing our wedding plans? I'm trying to catch Jeremy's eye, but he's too busy glaring at Richard. I tune everyone out and finish my soup. We should have more courses in our meals at home. Jeremy must think Mom and I are barbaric. All this time I've been trying to get him to loosen up when I should have been learning from him. We could be sort of elegant on a budget.

"Is that so?" Gordon's voice startles me, but I don't realize his question was actually directed to me until my mom says my name.

"I'm sorry … um … Gordon … sir, could you repeat that?" (Why am I just now realizing I don't know how I should address him?)

Gordon shows no sign I've insulted him. In fact, he might be slightly smiling—it's hard to tell because he has such deeply ingrained frown lines.

"Your mother tells me you have a degree in marketing?"

"Oh. Yes. But just a BS, not an MBA." (Do they even call those degrees by the same names here?) And how did a discussion of London's tourist spots veer to my education, anyway?

"Interesting that you and your mother both work with finances," Gordon says.

"Quite interesting," Richard adds.

I don't get his tone and glance at Jeremy for a clue, but he's glaring at his brother again.

"But, now, you write novels?" Gordon asks.

"She also handles the marketing for our business." Jeremy sounds like he's making a point in argument. "She's both intuitive and skilled in that."

Richard sneers at Jeremy. "Your business?"

"Yes, Richard. Chancing Press is a limited liability corporation."

Invisible weapons are definitely drawn at that end of the table.

"Isn't that lovely?" Amanda lays one hand on each of her sons' arms.

"I don't believe you mentioned the incorporation," Gordon says. "Are you finding the American business law a challenge?"

"Not at all," Jeremy says. "For the most part, it's based on British law."

"Ah. Well, then."

Luckily, the next course is served and we all grow quiet for a couple of minutes. As I eat, I watch Jeremy. Finally, he looks up at me, and I get a smile. A weak one. His jaw looks so tense I'm surprised he can chew. I think I've missed some subtext to the conversation around this table. Well, except for Richard's brattiness. I get that. And there he goes, breaking the silence.

"After dinner, dear brother, will you favor us with your playing?"

Another glare from Jeremy.

"Oh, please do," Amanda says.

Playing?

So yeah. Jeremy plays piano. Jeremy plays piano very well. But I'm doing great at hiding the fact I had no idea he plays, so it's all cool.

"Oh, Jeremy, that was beautiful," Mom says when he finishes his piece. "I had no idea you played. Did you, Chelsea?"

Jeremy keeps me from deciding whether to lie. "Thank you, Marie, but since we don't have a piano at home, I didn't feel it worth mentioning."

"Well, we're going to remedy that," she says like a piano is something she'll pick up on her next trip to Target.

We're having drinks and coffee in what the Pearces call their family room. It's the first room we sat in this afternoon. The one with the wall of photos. When, at Amanda's urging, Jeremy begins to play a second piece, I get up and move toward the photos. I'm anxious to see if there's anything else I don't know about my fiancé.

Yep. There is. He's wearing glasses in the photos taken when he was a child. He doesn't wear glasses now or even contacts—I'd have noticed. And there he is with Laura, both teens, dressed in fancy riding clothes and sitting on what looks like twin horses. And there he's in ski gear. Probably in the Alps. Or maybe somewhere more exotic. Speaking of exotic, here's a photo of the whole family posed in front of the Taj Mahal. Another of them looks like it's in some Asian setting, a Buddhist temple maybe. And there are several shots of the Pearce children, at various ages, taken in tropical locales.

"I'd be happy to show you the family albums, if you like," Amanda says from behind me.

When I turn toward her, I see that Jeremy has finished playing. I didn't even hear the music stop.

"Yes, I'd like that. Jeremy's seen all my childhood photos, but he had none to show me."

"We have hundreds. I'll get some copied for you, dear." Amanda smiles as she looks at the wall behind me. "He's quite photogenic, don't you think?"

"Totally." Why did Jeremy give me the wrong impression of her? She doesn't seem coldhearted to me. I've seen that smile on my mom. It's a proud mother's smile.

Jeremy's watching us intently. When he realizes I'm looking at him, he beckons me over. Yeah, like I'm going to just walk away from his mother.

"Well," she says. "I suppose we should rejoin the others."

Wow. It almost makes you believe it's true that mothers have eyes in the backs of their heads.

Ethan left after dinner … well, after the obligatory after-dinner coffee, which to his credit he drank rather than opting for more liquor like the other men. I can't believe how much these people drink. We sit around talking, mostly about the places the Pearces have traveled to, which is a subject Mom brought up. I've missed parts of the discussion because I'm trying to think what I'll say if they ask me about my world travels—which are nonexistent. This is my first trip outside the United States, well, except for a couple of trips to Mexico, and that's so close to home, I'm not sure that counts. My mom traveled to a few interesting places, at least, before she had us kids.

Luckily, no one asks me, and I'm relieved when it's time for bed.

Mom will be sleeping in a bedroom on the second floor— or whatever number they've assigned it—but the rest of us are on the floor above that. Except for Uncle Bert who has a "cottage" on the grounds, which, in Pearce terms, probably means a six-bedroom house. Jeremy and I are in his old room. He says Amanda moved the kids up here when they were teens so she could take over most of the second floor to create a master suite. You'd have to see that suite to believe it. I've seen it. Her dressing room alone is bigger than our bedroom at home. Her dressing room. I'm hoping to sneak around to snap photos of all the rooms in this house. Gabi will freak when she sees them.

Anyway.

This weekend, Jeremy, Laura, and Richard will be staying in the same rooms they slept in when they all still lived here. They even had their own, like, common room with a media center and kitchenette, making this whole floor a kind of dorm. I don't know how much time they spent here though. The way Jeremy tells it, they spent most of their time at boarding schools. I haven't seen Laura's and Richard's rooms, but Jeremy's room is way bigger than ours at home. It even has a fireplace, but I think that's a holdover from when the house was first built. It's warm in this house, but there was only one fireplace burning downstairs, so that was probably just for ambience. In my quest to learn all I didn't already know about Jeremy, I'm itching to examine every bit of this room, but he has other ideas. He's kissing my neck as he guides me toward the bed.

"Does Richard have his own place or does he still live with your parents?"

Jeremy puts a hand over my mouth. "Could we not talk about him at the moment? Or ever."

Sigh. He has only one thing on his mind. I grab his wrist and do this awesome leverage and spin move so he ends up flat on the bed with me on top of him. He looks startled for a moment. Then he grins.

"All right, girl, show me what you've got."

"You can't handle what I've got."

"Then I shall die happy."

I sit up, straddling his thighs. "Close your eyes."

"I'd rather look at you."

"Close your eyes and use your imagination, Mr. Writer." He closes them. "No peeking."

"You haven't got into sadism without telling me, have you?"

"Hush."

For a moment, I sit quietly admiring the handsome man beneath me. My treasure. With my fingernail barely touching, I trace over his eyelids, down the length of his nose, across his top lip, and then the bottom. His breath slows. He lies still. Slowly, I unbutton his shirt, brushing my lips across the skin as I uncover it. I unbutton his jeans and pull his shirttails loose. Grasping his collar, I lift him to sit and strip off his shirt. His eyelids flutter.

"Quit peeking."

I lay him back down. I wait until I'm sure he's keeping his eyes closed before I rake my nails lightly over his shoulders and down his biceps and across his nipples and down his stomach. His groan satisfies me, empowers me. I start over, this time raking his skin with more pressure. He takes a deep shuddery breath. I slip further down his thighs so I can run my tongue around his navel, while I slide down his zipper.

"Wait," he says, his voice a husky whisper. He's breathing hard now. His fingers tangle in my hair. "Wait."

"No."

I spring loose the object of my desire from the confines of his underwear.

eleven

I wake again just before dawn. With all the liquor and wine and food I consumed last night, I didn't sleep well. I got spooked one of the times I woke. A strange noise started me thinking about how old and how big this house is, and I wondered if it might be haunted. Then I worried it was a ghost that kept waking me, so I spent the rest of the night with my head under the covers and my body pressed against Jeremy's.

Now, after scanning the room for any unwanted visitors, I tiptoe to the window to catch the sunrise. Sometimes I miss being awake when most of the world is still sleeping—not that I miss waking that early to go work in a deli, which is where I worked when I first met Jeremy. But I miss the peacefulness. At home, Mom is always awake before I am, unless she's sick, so there's no time for quiet morning thoughts alone.

Standing at this window at the top of the house, surrounded by silence, is even better than driving alone through mostly deserted streets. As the sky lightens, the grounds come into view, shrouded in mist tinted pink by the first glow of sunrise. It's breathtaking. Jeremy was so lucky to grow up in such a beautiful place.

He stirs behind me. "What are you doing up so early?"

"I wanted to see the sunrise. Come look. It's so gorgeous and romantic, like that scene in the movie Pride and Prejudice when Keira and Matthew see each other across the misty moor."

"You're not looking at a moor. And since when are you an Austen fan?"

His grumpiness surprises me, but I choose to ignore it. "You know I love that movie. You watched it with me and Mom just last month." He says nothing, so I turn back to the window. The light is now coloring the mist golden. A movement below draws my eye. "Oh. Isn't that your uncle?"

Jeremy gets out of bed to peer over my head. "Yes, it is … apparently on the way to his cottage."

"But I thought he slept in his cottage last night."

Jeremy pulls me back against him and whispers in my ear. "You're very sexy in the morning."

"No, you're just very horny in the morning. And don't we need to get showered and dressed?"

"Precisely my thought." He pulls me away from the window. "To the shower with us."

The kitchen of Dovewood House shocks me. It's not only the largest one I've ever seen, but it's also completely modernized. A dining table sits at the far end, in a large alcove with floor-to-ceiling windows and glass doors offering a spectacular 180-degree view of the grounds. The room glows with the natural light plus chandeliers and recessed spotlights all illuminating pale sand-colored stone countertops and floor, beige walls, white cabinetry—scads of it—and stainless steel appliances. I can't imagine this looks anything like the original kitchen.

Amanda, Gordon, Uncle Bert, and Mom are engrossed in conversation around the table. A short older woman stands at the stove, evidently the Mrs. Flynn Jeremy's told me about. But surely she's not cooking more for this meal because there's already a dozen dishes displayed on the breakfast bar. I'm relieved to see this meal is a casual buffet.

Jeremy takes my hand, and we walk up behind Mrs. Flynn. He taps her on the shoulder. When she turns around, her face lights up.

"Here's me dear boy." She lays down her wooden spoon to clasp his face between her hands. "Say you missed me cooking, even if that's a lie."

"Indeed I do miss it, as well as your smiles. But don't you worry. I'm being well fed at home."

She lets him go and folds her hands above her stomach as she looks me over. "By this pretty one?"

"Yes, and her mother, Marie." He puts his arm around my shoulders. "Mrs. Flynn, I'd like you to meet my fiancée, Chelsea Cole."

I hold out my hand. "It's nice to meet you. I've heard a lot of great things about your cooking."

Mrs. Flynn swats away my words, but she's beaming. She takes my hand in both of hers and leans close so she can speak quietly. "I'm being forever grateful if you make me dear boy happy for the rest of his life."

"That's my plan."

She winks at me, and then she turns back to the stove and picks up her spoon. "I've got your favorite dish planned for tonight."

"Which one?" Jeremy asks.

She chuckles and shoos him away. "You and the miss eat your breakfast now."

"Yes, ma'am."

I follow Jeremy's lead and fill a plate from the buffet spread. I'm a little mystified by Mrs. Flynn's display of affection toward him. Surely she's not a relative or he wouldn't call her Mrs. But then, I'm already confused by the Pearce family relationships. I'll have to ask him about her later.

"Did you sleep well?" Amanda asks.

When Jeremy doesn't respond, I do. "Very well, thank you. I got up early to watch the sunrise." Jeremy nudges me with his knee. Did I say something wrong?

"It's peaceful waking here in the country." Amanda laughs lightly. "It's peaceful here all the time, I suppose. The city can be so stressful."

"Not for Gordon," Uncle Bert says. "He thrives on it."

"Some of us have no choice," Gordon grumbles.

I sense reproof, but I don't know why. And my mom, ever vigilant to avoid discord, jumps in.

"I can't wait to take a walk around your beautiful grounds."

Uncle Bert grins. "It will be my pleasure to act as your guide, Marie."

I'm still looking at Gordon, so I catch the dark look he shoots at Uncle Bert. I feel like I've missed something. Maybe they argued before Jeremy and I came downstairs. If so, whatever was said doesn't seem to have bothered Uncle Bert. I wish Laura had been at the table; she'd clue me in.

A few minutes later, Gordon stands. "If you'll excuse me, I have a few phone calls to make. Jeremy, I'd like you to come to my study when you've finished eating." He's already turning toward the door when he adds, "If you will."

♥

Laura and I are sitting in the sun on the terrace. When she came down to the kitchen and found out Jeremy was with his father, she decided to bring her coffee and toast breakfast outside. At her invitation, we left Richard and Amanda alone in the kitchen.

She chooses a lounge and turns it to face the sun. "So. Did Dad give Jeremy any indication what he wanted to discuss with him?"

I shake my head. "All I know is that Jeremy looked like he'd been ordered to the gallows. I don't really get it. So far I haven't seen any of the drama I expected here … except from Jeremy."

"Do you think he has regrets about leaving his position with the law firm?"

My heart clenches. "Not that he's mentioned to me. Just the opposite, actually. Why? Has he said that to you?"

"No." She sips her coffee. "He always sounds content when we talk on the phone, but he's … I don't know, he seems different now that he's home."

She's brushing crumbs off her lap, so if the pain of hearing her refer to England as Jeremy's home shows on my face, she doesn't see it. I know she meant nothing by it, but it's what I fear he's thinking too.

"I nearly choked last night at dinner when you described Jeremy as shy," she says.

"Your father seemed surprised too, but when I first met Jeremy—" My mouth drops open. "Do you think that was just an act?"

Laura looks past me. "Ask him."

"Ask me what?" Jeremy says.

Think quick. "What did your father want?"

"He offered to hold our wedding here. I told him absolutely no."

"Well … we couldn't. I mean none of my guests could afford to come. And even Gabi … not with a newborn."

"As I said, I declined."

"You were with him a long time. Is that all he wanted?"

He shrugs. "It was nothing important. Do you mind if I swim laps for a while?"

"Um … no." Without another word, he turns and heads back into the house. I look at Laura. "What was that?"

"I'd say the 'nothing important' he and Dad discussed necessitates a need to release tension or consider—"

"An ultimatum?"

"I was going to say consider a different offer."

For a moment, we sit with only birdsong breaking the silence. I gaze across the lawn that seems to stretch for a mile before it ends at a stone wall. "Your parents don't want Jeremy to marry me, do they?"

Laura sits up in her chair. "Why do you think that?"

"How did they react when they found out we were engaged?"

"Surprised, of course, and … well, I won't deny they were upset with him for not telling them sooner. And, naturally, they were curious about you. Still are, which is why you were invited here, of course."

"But they must be unhappy that I'm not in the same social class as … well … you all."

Laura rolls her eyes as she picks up her cup. "We are not who you're referring to." She takes a sip of coffee. "To be honest, I don't think Mum ever believed Jeremy would marry she-who-will-not-be named. That was Dad's hope. He has some throwback gene, thinking he's supposed to marry off his children like a king creating political alliances or something."

"Which means he can't be happy about Jeremy marrying me."

"Don't worry about him." When her phone vibrates against the glass tabletop, she picks it up and looks at the screen. "Excuse me. I need to take this."

I get up and go back into the kitchen. "Where's your mother?" I ask Richard.

"Why do you want to know?" I stare him down until he gives in. "She's in her sitting room."

Amanda's door stands open. The morning light bathes the room in a cheerful rosy glow. Classical music plays softly. When I knock, she turns from the window and smiles at me. "Come in, Chelsea. Is Jeremy still with Gordon?"

"No, he's swimming laps."

"Oh dear."

"That's a bad sign, huh?"

She sighs and motions for us to sit on the sofa. "It probably means they argued. Did he tell you what they talked about?"

"Not everything, but he said Gordon offered to hold our wedding here."

"Which you've declined."

"Yes, but I wanted to thank you for the offer and explain why we can't do that. I'm sure you know that my mother and I aren't … we don't have … we're not …" I can't stop myself from glancing around the room.

She pats my hand, just like my mom does. "It wouldn't be

financially feasible to fly your entire wedding party and guests here. I completely understand and told Gordon that."

"I didn't want you to think I wasn't grateful for the offer. This would be an awesome place for a wedding."

"Well, perhaps we'll find out with Laura. Or Richard. But I wonder if you might let us plan a sort of second wedding reception for you. In June, perhaps?"

"Do you think Jeremy will agree to that?"

Her eyes widen. Then she smiles. "I'm sure you could persuade him."

"Us living on two continents is a problem, isn't it?"

"Not one we can't manage."

For a moment, the only sounds are violins and cellos, and I wonder if I've been dismissed. I'm just about to stand when Amanda speaks again.

"I've read the Penny James books." The sparkle in her eyes matches her smile. "I quite enjoyed them. I hope that confession doesn't make you uncomfortable."

"Me? No. I'm glad you told me. But ..." Amanda lifts her brows expectantly. "Well, does that mean you no longer disapprove of Jeremy wanting to be a writer?"

Her face slackens in surprise. "Disapprove?"

"Um ... well, I got the impression you and Gordon had forbidden him to—"

"Forbidden." With a hand splayed at her throat, she shakes her head. "I believe it's been ten years since I forbade Jeremy anything. As for Gordon"—she sighs again—"those two have locked heads since Jeremy learned to speak. Unfortunately, that cast me in the role of mediator far too often. And at times Jeremy has blamed me, accused me of not trying hard enough to change his father's mind."

"That must be tough."

She seems about to respond, but her phone's ringing interrupts. "Excuse me." She goes to her desk and checks the caller ID. "I'm sorry, Chelsea, but I've been waiting for this call."

"No problem."

Amanda answers the call, but before I leave the room she asks the caller to wait a minute. "Chelsea," she says, "did Jeremy tell you we had forbidden him to write?"

Uh-oh. "I think … well, maybe … probably I just got the wrong impression."

She nods, but I have a feeling she knows I lied.

I walk directly to the indoor pool. Jeremy is still swimming laps, but more leisurely than I expected. Maybe he's cooled off. I stand on the coping at the end of the pool, waiting for him to reach me. When he surfaces to turn, he stops and lifts his swim goggles to the top of his head.

"What did you argue with your father about?"

"I told you."

"You told me only part of it."

He sighs. "Could we not talk about this now?"

"When will we?"

His jaw tightens. "It's really not your concern."

"Seriously? We're doing that again?"

"Doing what?"

"Hiding things from each other?"

He says nothing. After a moment, he pulls down his goggles and swims away from me. I can't believe it. I stomp to the end of the pool he's headed for, but then I keep going. Along this whole end of the pool room are floor-to-ceiling windows and French doors, like in the kitchen, so I can see Laura still sitting outside. I exit to the patio. Terrace. Whatever.

"Where did you go?" she asks.

"I wanted to thank your mother for the wedding offer."

"And she angered you?"

"What? No. Jeremy did that. He won't tell me what he argued about with your father."

"Leave it. He'll get over it." She closes her eyes and tilts her face up to the sun.

"Did you know your mother's read our books?"

"Of course."

"Does Jeremy know?"

She opens one eye and squints at me. "Not from me. I doubt Mum told him either. Like your mum, she'd feel uncomfortable."

"But he thinks she's against his decision to write."

Now she opens both eyes and looks directly at me. "I don't see how that could be true. She's always known his heart wasn't in practicing law. That's why she encouraged him toward the arts … behind Dad's back. Of course, she hoped he'd take music more seriously, but—"

"I didn't even know he played."

"Yes, I guessed that when your mother commented on his piano at my place."

"I'm starting to worry there's a lot I don't know about him."

Laura leans toward me, concern creasing her forehead. "What's important is his character, and after living together for months, I can't imagine you don't know that."

"You're right. I do know him. And I'm sure he'll tell me what they talked about when he's calmed down." I start to sit down, but realize that despite the sun, I'm freezing. "I'm going inside to get a jacket."

"When Jeremy's finished with the pool, we'll show you the grounds."

"Great."

I cross the patio. Before I step back inside, I can see that the pool is empty. I continue around the pool toward the doors into the hall, but stop when I realize I can hear Jeremy's voice faintly. It's coming from the changing room, I think, so I edge closer. I hear only his voice. He's on the phone.

"… getting sucked into all this." Pause. "And that's why I didn't want to bring her here, Ethan." Pause. "Worse. It's going much worse than I feared." Pause. "Of course he noticed. That's why he brought it up." Pause. "I know. I know. Look, get your arse on the move and come rescue me." Pause. "Right."

Those last words were louder, meaning Jeremy's moving toward me. I scurry through the doors to the reception hall and run up to our bedroom. I go straight to the windows, giving me a view of the patio below. Jeremy's outside now, talking to Laura. When he glances up toward this room, I duck back and drop down into the nearby chair.

So. Jeremy didn't want to bring me here. And what does he think is worse than he feared? Me? My behavior? And I'm so obviously out of their class that his father noticed and … what? Told him to call off the wedding? Oh, shut up, Chelsea. That makes no sense. Right. Amanda knew about the offer to have our wedding here, so obviously Gordon wasn't telling Jeremy to end our relationship.

But there's one thing I got straight—Jeremy wants to be rescued from being here with me.

♥

Laura and Jeremy show me the outdoor pool and pool house, the tennis court, and the formal gardens. They share with me some of their memories at each of those places. Most of those stories are hilarious, but still I sense sadness in Jeremy. I guess it could just be that nostalgia I feel when I remember my childhood, but I don't think so. I think he's realizing how much he misses swimming in that pool and playing on that court, even if he could only do that on family weekends. Yet he holds my hand, doing a good job of acting like nothing's wrong.

We pass Uncle Bert's cottage, which is much larger than the groundskeeper's cottage they point out at the far edge of a meadow, but not as large as I'd imagined. We walk only a bit into the woods, where Laura searches for the early spring wildflowers, and Jeremy tells me about the summer he was nine and deliberately got Richard lost here and suffered the punishment of "no pudding" for a month. (Though I'm sure he sweet-talked Mrs. Flynn into secretly giving him some.)

Finally, we arrive at the stable. As soon as we enter, a black horse whinnies, and Jeremy goes straight to it. The horse lays his head on Jeremy's shoulder, and he wraps an arm around its neck. A horse hug. And that's obviously Jeremy's horse. Another thing he's given up for me.

My mom's laughter draws my attention. Flushed and giddy, she's just ridden up to the stable with Uncle Bert. Her hair is windblown, making her look younger and carefree. I'm happy for her.

"Oh, that was fun," she cries as they walk their horses inside. "I'd forgotten how much I loved riding. You have to try it, Chelsea."

"I'm pretty sure putting me on a horse would not be a good thing, Mom."

"You can handle it," Jeremy says.

"But—"

"Stardust would be the best choice, eh, Rupert?" Uncle Bert says.

A white-haired man, still powerfully built, steps out of the shadows. "She would, Albert."

Jeremy takes my hand and pulls me toward the man who's moved to a stall holding a speckled gray horse, Stardust, I presume. "Mr. Flynn, I'd like you to meet my fiancée, Chelsea Cole."

He pulls off his cap and bows his head. "Miss."

"Are you related to Mrs. Flynn?" I ask him.

"Married forty-six years."

"Oh, wow. Congratulations."

He nods and replaces his hat.

"Rupert there is as skilled in the stable as Tilly is in the kitchen," Uncle Bert says. Mr. Flynn waves away the compliment, just like his wife did, and enters the stall.

"Black Jack could do with some exercise," he tells Jeremy.

So. It seems I'm going to ride a horse for the first time today. I stand idly with Laura and watch as Mr. Flynn saddles Stardust and Jeremy saddles his horse. "Aren't you coming with us?" I ask her.

"And intrude on your romantic ride through a sun-dappled meadow?"

"Somehow I see a different scenario playing out."

Mr. Flynn motions me over. He takes my hand and places it on the horse's nose. "Stroke her," he says. "Say her name. Get comfortable with her."

"Comfortable. Right." I do as he says, hoping she's more at ease with me than I am with her. How badly could I get hurt falling from this horse? Surely Jeremy's not risking my life. His bad mood seems to have lifted, but still I'm worried about what I overheard him say to Ethan.

Laura helps me adjust my riding helmet, and then, too soon, Jeremy's boosting me up onto Stardust.

"Hold these, thumbs up," he says, placing the reins in my hands. "Relax but keep your back straight. Don't lean forward." The horse shuffles, and I squeeze its sides with my knees. "No. Don't do that. Relax."

"I'm sitting ten-feet high on a horse, Jeremy. How relaxed do you expect me to be?"

"Ten feet," he scoffs. He pulls my foot back in the stirrup. "Keep the ball of your foot here, heels down."

"You'll be fine," my mom says.

"Stardust's gentle enough for a child," Uncle Bert adds.

Perfect. I feel like a five-year-old.

Jeremy leads our horses out of the stable, and then he mounts his like he's been doing it all his life, which he has. "She'll follow my lead," he says as the horses start off walking around the fenced pasture. If I wasn't so freaked, I might enjoy this. "Relax," he says for the millionth time.

I take a deep breath, and we continue circling the pasture.

"Ethan will be here in a while," he says. "We're going to lunch in the village."

"Oh. Okay."

"Do you mind?"

"No, that's fine. I'll have lunch with your family."

"By we, I meant you, me, and Laura."

"Oh. Yes, that sounds nice." Okay. So maybe he wasn't telling Ethan he needs to be rescued from me.

I'm startled when Stardust shakes her head, but I keep my balance. I'm just getting the hang of this when the horses speed up. "Wait. Why do we have to go so fast?"

Jeremy laughs. "This is only a trot. Move with it."

"Move what?"

"Your hips. Feel the horse's rhythm and rock them with it."

Jeremy watches as I try my best. "There you go," he says. "Now don't tense again."

"Why? What are you going to do?"

He slows the horses and walks us over to the gate leading to the big meadow. When he jumps off Black Jack, I panic and almost fall off Stardust. He just laughs and shakes his head.

"I'm glad you find this funny."

"I do. It's hilarious that someone who can balance on a surfboard in a ten-foot wave is afraid of sitting on a horse."

He guides the horses through the gate, closes it, and swings back up in his saddle. We start off at a trot this time. I focus on the movement, and I'm doing okay until Jeremy does something to make the horses start racing across the meadow. I'm screaming. He's laughing.

"It's too fast," I yell.

"Don't be a wimp. This is only a canter."

We cut across the meadow and then circle it. I've stopped screaming because I need to breathe. During the fourth lap, I realize my girly parts are warming from all this saddle rocking. As we come back around to the edge of the woods, Jeremy slows and guides Black Jack onto the path leading into them. Stardust follows.

"Why are we going into the woods?"

"I have something to show you."

"What?"

"Something new."

"Is this the same trick you played on Richard?"

He laughs. "I assure you it's not."

Two minutes later, we're half naked, and he is indeed teaching me something new. Okay, so it's definitely not me he wants to be rescued from.

When Ethan arrives, we drive to the village. I can't help getting all googly-eyed at the sight of it. I jump out of the car as soon as it stops.

"It's so old and beautiful. I want to walk around and see everything."

"That's sure to kill two minutes," Jeremy says.

He wasn't far wrong, though we walked only around the square and through the little park. They balked at showing me the cemetery. It's weird how quaint everything looks, like I've stepped back in time. That picture is disturbed only when I notice modern details like the free Wi-Fi sign in front of the small inn. When we enter a dark little pub that looks like it's been here for hundreds of years, I'm relieved not to see a huge LED TV tuned to some soccer match.

"Now, lads, mind yourselves," the bartender calls out when we walk in.

"Ack, Dave," Ethan says, "Can't you see we're with ladies?"

He grins. "I do indeed. Pretty ones too."

"So nice to see you home, Jeremy," a plump, red-haired woman calls out.

"Thank you, Mrs. Clarke," Jeremy answers with a smile.

"How's the judge, young Pearce?" asks an elderly man at the bar.

"He's fine, sir," Jeremy answers.

"I saw your lovely mum, a week Tuesday. We talked about the festival."

Jeremy nods.

"And your parents, young Grant?"

Ethan holds up three fingers. "Mum's married again. Dad's retiring."

The old man clucks his tongue and shakes his head like Ethan's just told him they're both dying, then turns back to his pint without another word.

"Who is that?" I whisper to Jeremy.

"Mr. Dolan, the mayor," he says absently. He's focused on the blackboard behind the bar. "Lamb stew; egg and chips; sausage and onion sandwich; grilled chicken wrap; burger and chips; corned beef and pickle ciabatta," he reads. "And the classic cheese and pickle, naturally."

"They make all that here?" The place is so small; I can't imagine it has a kitchen.

He points toward the door. "Brought in from Decker's."

"The restaurant down the street," Laura explains. "All tasty."

"Why didn't we just go to the restaurant?"

"No on-license," Ethan says.

"No alcohol," Jeremy translates.

Of course.

After lunch, we walk a bit more. We end up back in the park. Ethan and Laura are playing like kids on the slide ... a chute, they call it. Jeremy and I each took one turn, but now we're sitting on a bench, snuggling and watching them. My phone rings. It's Gabi. I calculate the time difference and freak when I realize it's the middle of the night in California. I jump to my feet as I tap to answer.

"You're not in labor, are you?"

"Hello to you too, Chels. And no, I'm not in labor. I can't sleep and decided to call you since we've had trouble connecting up with this stupid time difference."

"Yeah, I know." I return to the bench. "We've just had lunch and now we're sitting in the park in the middle of this village straight out of Austen. You would love it."

"How's it going with his parents?"

"Um … good. Laura's here too. And Ethan came to take us to lunch."

"You're in the country, right?"

"Yes, and oh, Gabi, you wouldn't believe their house. It's a mansion called Dovewood. I'll take photos of everything and send them to you. It's just so beautiful you can't imagine." I flash a smile at Jeremy, but he's looking straight ahead, his face stony. "And get this, they have horses and I rode one. Can you believe that?"

"You on a horse?"

"Damn straight, and I didn't fall off or anything."

"So Dovewood's a mansion for real?"

"Totally. And it's been in his family for centuries. But it's modernized, of course. We had a tour. Two swimming pools, a kitchen to die for, and you should see his mother's dressing room."

"How many rooms in the house?"

"A lot. Wait." I turn to Jeremy. "How many rooms are—" Jeremy snatches the phone out of my hand.

"She'll call you later, Gabi." He clicks off and lays my phone on the bench between us.

"What the hell?" He stares straight ahead. "I can't believe you did that."

"You were being rude."

"Seriously? Rude is grabbing someone's phone and ending the call. What's your problem?"

"We're here with others," he says, not even looking at me. "Taking a casual phone call signals that you have no interest in your company."

I've embarrassed him. Now even he sees me as having no class. I blink back tears. My phone is vibrating on the bench, no doubt with a text from Gabi. I won't dare pick it up.

After a few minutes of silence, Jeremy picks up my phone and reads her text, then hits the call icon. "Gabi, I'm the one who ended the call, and I apologize for that." Pause. "Temporary insanity, I suppose. In any case, here's Chelsea." He stands and hands the phone to me.

As I take it from him, he turns and walks toward Ethan who's pushing Laura on a swing.

"What the hell does he mean by temporary insanity?" Gabi says.

"I don't know." And I truly don't, but I'm pretty sure it can't be good.

twelve

Jeremy woke before I did, but even though it's more than an hour until breakfast, he's not in our bedroom or bathroom. Worried that I've forgotten about some traditional Pearce Saturday-morning event and overslept, I get ready for the day in record time.

I've never walked through the house this early in the morning. The third floor hall and stairwell are lit only with nightlights, I guess you'd call them, spaced about ten feet apart along the baseboards. I wonder if one of the servants has the job to turn on the house lights at appropriate times. As I reach the bottom of the stairs, a glow from the reception hall draws my attention. It's coming through the French doors that lead to the indoor pool. And there's Jeremy, standing on the pool deck.

I head that way. When I'm a few feet closer, my field of vision widens, and I realize he's not alone. He's with his mother. I take a giant step as far as I can to the left, hopefully out of view, and tiptoe up to stand in the dark peeking through the edge of a windowpane. They're both dressed in swimsuits and water is puddled at their feet. I wonder if this pre-dawn swim used to be a ritual with them.

Although they're facing each other, I don't think Jeremy's looking directly at her. Amanda is taller than me, but still several inches shorter than Jeremy, so though his head is bent, it's also turned slightly to the side. He's not in his outraged or even his defensive posture, so I don't get the sense that they're arguing. But why is he not meeting her eyes?

Amanda's mouth is moving, but I can hear only a murmur, not well enough to make out any words. Once or twice, Jeremy nods. She lifts her hand to Jeremy's chin and turns his face toward hers. Then she lays her palm against his cheek and leans in to say something. He nods again. Then he hugs her. She returns the hug, rubbing his back when he doesn't release her right away.

I know I'm witnessing some reconciliation between them, but I also know that if he doesn't tell me about it, I can't ask him without revealing I spied on them. They break apart, and he puts his arm around her shoulders as they walk together toward the changing room.

When the chandelier in the reception hall comes on, I jump, sure I've been caught. But no one is in the room. Apparently, either the lights are automated or there's a master switch somewhere. Where do I go now? I check the time on my phone. It's still too early to go to the kitchen. I rush back upstairs and into our room. I figure I can hide in the bathroom and when I hear Jeremy open the bedroom door, I'll come out and pretend I just finished getting ready. But two seconds later, he enters.

I turn toward him. "You're up early."

With a glance, he notes that I'm fully clothed with hair and makeup already done. "And so are you."

"Your hair is wet."

"I went for a swim. And now I'm going to shower." He takes a step toward the bathroom.

"Did you swim alone?"

He pauses but doesn't look at me. "My mother was there."

Before I can say another word, he's in the bathroom and closing the door. My confusion about his relationship with his mother, at least, remains. Why does he want me to think she's rejected him, when everything I've seen and heard contradicts that?

But most of all, I don't understand why he's shutting me out.

The last two days have been a roller coaster with Jeremy. Mostly he's sullen, especially when his father or Richard is around, though I don't see any tenderness with his mom again either. He lightens up if we're with Laura or Ethan or Uncle Bert or Mom. But with me, he's not himself at all. I mean, he hasn't done anything freaky like grabbing my phone again, but one minute he seems almost desperate for my approval and the next it's like he wishes I weren't around. And though he avoids any real conversation between us by insisting the only problem is that he'd just rather be in the city, he keeps looking at me all sad. When I catch him, he tries to cover it with a smile, but I'm not fooled. And get this—we haven't had sex since that quickie in the woods on Friday. That says a lot. *A lot.*

Now we're having one last family lunch before we head back to London. I'm not in the best mood. This whatever-it-is between Jeremy and me has my nerves on edge. And Richard is droning on and on about work because he thinks that makes him look like the favored son.

"I've read the briefs on the Claymoore suit," he says to Gordon. "I believe I could handle that. Do you think I should approach Leon about it?"

Gordon doesn't even look up from his plate."I think you should refer to your superiors in less familiar terms, Richard. And be thankful for the work you're given and perform it to the best of your ability."

"But Jeremy was handling cases like—"

"Richard." Gordon looks at him now, signaling he's done with that conversation.

Richard looks crushed.

"You'll have your life stolen by the practice soon enough, Richard," Uncle Bert says, smiling. "Enjoy your freedom while you can."

Gordon glares at Uncle Bert.

It's clear to me now that Richard's not favored at all. He's tolerated. Tolerated by Gordon, that is. I think Amanda feels sorry for him because Richard wants so badly to measure up to Jeremy in his father's eyes—like Gordon is some god— which is ironic, when you think about it, because Jeremy thinks he's nothing in his father's eyes. Just thinking about that makes me furious.

"You're a very insecure man, aren't you?" I say.

Total silence. Please, God, let me melt right through the floor. I swear I didn't mean to say that out loud. To Gordon. If you flashed a photo of this scene in this instant you'd think everyone at the table except me was a mannequin. I glance across the table at my mom. She's staring at me, but I think there's a hint of a smile in her eyes. I wish I could say the same for Gordon's. His eyes tell me he not only can't believe I said what I did, but that I'm scum for saying it.

And that really ticks me off. I'm tired of trying to be someone I'm not. Trying to win the almighty Gordon's approval. Now I understand how Jeremy feels—only he's been feeling it his whole life. I stand and face him.

"If you weren't insecure, you'd be proud of Jeremy for doing what he loves and doing it well. Instead, you punish him for not living up to your expectations. For not being a carbon copy of you." I drop my napkin on the table. "Well, you should know that Jeremy's not only a successful writer, but he's a wonderful man."

I don't stay around to face the aftermath. I'm out of the dining room and starting up the stairs before it hits me that I've probably made the biggest mistake of my life. I've just totally disrespected the man my fiancé wants to accept and love him. I'm despicable. Jeremy will never marry me now.

In our room, I stand at the window looking out over the beautiful landscape I'll never see again. What makes me even sadder is that, in the eyes of Jeremy's parents, I've also disgraced my mother, and she doesn't deserve that a bit. She must be furious with me, or she would have joined me up here by now. *Crap.* I've ruined her romance with Uncle Bert too. He may be the nicer brother, but he's still a Pearce. He'll have to stick with Gordon. *Gasp.* What if Mom sticks with the Pearces too?

I start packing. I've emptied two drawers before I accept that what I really need to do is go back downstairs and apologize—to everyone. I spoke the truth, so I'm not sorry for what I said, just that I said it. Or maybe just the way I said it.

But I'm a guest in their home, and rudeness to your host is not excusable. I leave the suitcase on the bed and swallow my pride. And boy does that feel as big as a watermelon.

The dining room is already being cleared, so I go to the family room. I stand outside the open door for a minute trying to hear the conversation, but it's too muffled. Then I hear someone laugh, and I know my mother isn't in the room—at least I hope she's not sitting there allowing someone to laugh at me. Taking a deep breath, I walk in. I look for Jeremy first. Disappointment crushes me when I see he's not there. Ohmygod. Neither is Gordon. He must be skinning Jeremy alive—for what I did.

Only Mom, Amanda, Laura, and Uncle Bert are in the room, drinking coffee. Richard's probably eavesdropping and smirking while Gordon lays into Jeremy.

"Come in, Chelsea," Amanda says. "Help yourself at the bar."

This is too weird. All four of them are smiling at me.

"I … I came down …" Deciding a drink is exactly what I need, I go to the bar and pour myself something brown. (How do these people know what's in these stupid decanters anyway?) I gulp it down. And it's obviously top shelf because it doesn't take my breath away.

"I came down to apologize for my rudeness." I'm facing Amanda, but I glance at everyone else so they know they're included.

"As the eldest in this room," Uncle Bert says solemnly, "I absolve you." Every crease on his face deepens as he breaks into a grin.

"But Gordon—"

"Absolves you too, I assure you."

"Your timing wasn't the best," Amanda says, "but your passion is commendable."

"But Gordon—"

"Is in his study."

"With Jeremy?"

"Yes, dear, and thank God. It's time they ended this alpha-male nonsense."

I drop into the nearest chair. "But what I said—"

"Was the truth," Laura says.

"But Jeremy—"

My mom reaches over and squeezes my hand. "Chelsea, sweetie, let it go. It will all work out fine."

That may be reasonable from their point of view. But they don't know that things have changed since we came to England. They don't know that Jeremy's changed his feelings about me. And my angering his father sure isn't going to help change them back.

I can't stand just sitting around waiting for Jeremy and Gordon to end their argument or finish their conversation or whatever it is they're doing, so I go back upstairs and finish packing. Laura's luggage is already sitting on the landing waiting to be taken downstairs, and Mom's has probably been in the entry hall since before breakfast. Jeremy hasn't come upstairs by the time I'm finished, so I set our bags beside Laura's and creep down the stairs.

I circle around the long way to the family room so I can pass Gordon's office. The door is open and the room empty. I move on and eavesdrop outside the family room. No one's shouting. Or crying. The conversation tone sounds normal. I take a deep breath and step inside.

Jeremy jumps to his feet when he sees me. "Would you like a drink?"

"No. I had one."

"Coffee?" Amanda says. "Or it's no problem to get you a cup of tea, if you'd like."

"I'm good." Amanda looks puzzled, so I change that to, "I'm fine."

"Come," Gordon says. "Sit and talk for a while before you leave for the city."

Okay. I get it. Come sit with us so we can tell you how rude and ungrateful you are. But after a few minutes, I realize they aren't going to say anything like that. It's just chitchat about the unusual amount of sun we had for this weekend and the traffic we'll probably encounter on the drive back and what we have planned for the next few days. I'm freaked that everyone is acting like lunch wasn't ruined by a psycho who means well. This family is more dysfunctional than I thought.

Jeremy even discusses something law related with his father without bristling. Richard joins us finally, and I realize he was probably only packing while Gordon was in his study with Jeremy.

Soon we're all standing outside, smiling and giving hugs and agreeing to meet for dinner on Friday. It's bizarre. When Richard steps forward to say goodbye, he gives me a hug— totally chaste—and whispers, "I'm sorry I insulted you when we first met."

"I accept that apology, Richard."

"Thank you." He steps back, half turning before he stops and looks at me again. "I really do like the law. And I'm going to be a success."

"Good to hear. But you don't have to compete with Jeremy anymore, you know?"

He nods.

Uncle Bert has offered to drive my mom and Laura back to London in his car—because of the luggage problem, he says, but it's obviously a ploy to give Jeremy and me time alone. Won't that be fun. I can tell by his eyes that he's about to flip into Mr. High Tea mode and lay into me.

But we drive for ten minutes in silence. As we're passing through the village, the sight of that park bench speeds up my heart and forces me to start the conversation.

"I'm sorry for my rudeness at lunch. I didn't mean to just blurt that out."

He glances at me, eyes wide. "That certainly took me by surprise."

"And I know how you just love it when I blurt out things."

I could swear the corners of his mouth curl up slightly, but he says nothing. We drive for a bit longer, both of us just staring ahead at the road. I've progressed to thinking he's decided never to speak to me again when he clears his throat.

"My father ... I wasn't, that is, I'"—raindrops spatter the windshield, and he turns on the wipers—"need to apologize to you."

"For what?"

"I'm responsible for your blurt." He turns his gaze from the road to me for barely a second, and then takes a deep breath. "My parents ... my father never actually forbade me to write."

"But you said—"

"I know. I know. That's what I'm apologizing for."

"So you're telling me I insulted your father for absolutely no reason?"

"Don't worry. I explained everything to him."

"You mean the story you told me about him backhanding you was a lie?"

"No. He did hit me, but … I may have provoked him."

"By telling him you wanted to be a writer."

"Well, that and also … I called him a few names." His glance is an appeal. "I told you I was drunk that night."

"Damn it, Jeremy. You did make it clear to your father that I had the wrong impression of him, right?"

"I told you I did."

He gives me a smile like everything's just peachy now. I don't return it. I look out my window like I'm just watching the scenery. He can't possible think I should just let this go and move on. Everything I know about his past is spinning in my head. What else have I got wrong? What else has he lied about?

"My father approves of you, if that's what you're worried about." His change of tone makes me turn back to him. "They want to throw some public spectacle for us after the wedding."

"A second reception, your mother said, for your family and friends who won't be at our wedding. I think that's a lovely gesture."

He shoots me an icy look before turning back to the road.

"And it appears to me that you'd have fewer problems with your father if you weren't instantly on the defense. You just assume he—"

"Assume?" He scoffs. "Do you know how he reacted when my mother told him about our engagement? He assumed you and your mother were only after the family money. His money."

Damn. I sit quietly reviewing my impression of Gordon. Wait. "Well, so what? Okay. He's obsessed with money. I'll give you that. But obviously he no longer suspects I'm a gold digger, or he would have told you to call off the wedding—not invited us to hold it here. That offer was extremely generous. If you didn't have a chip on your shoulder, you'd see that."

He slows the car and stares at me for a moment, shaking his head as if I'm totally ignorant. His jaw clenches as he turns away and speeds up even faster than he was driving before.

We don't speak for the rest of the drive.

Jeremy gets a text as we're unloading the cars at Laura's. "Ethan wants to know if we'll meet him at the pub at five," he says, looking straight at Laura.

She glances at me before saying, "Fine with me, but he invited us all, right?"

Uncle Bert whispers something to Mom.

"We have other plans," she says, blushing. "Dinner," she adds.

Hmm. I'm pretty sure Uncle Bert whispered more than a dinner invitation to her, so I'm not surprised when he kisses her on the cheek before getting back into his car. I look to see if Jeremy noticed, but he's already started toward the door with a load of luggage. I follow him with the rest of ours.

When Laura's and Mom's suitcases are sorted out on their floor, Jeremy and I carry the rest up to our room. "It's stuffy in here," he says and crosses the room to open a window.

Detecting an apologetic tone in his voice, I push back all the questions that formed during our drive. I just want to unpack, do a load of laundry, and go to the pub. Maybe by the time we go to bed tonight, things will be back to normal between us.

When I've finished emptying my suitcase, I realize Jeremy is still standing by the window, and that flips a switch to set my emotional alarm clanging. As if some poisonous vapor is floating in through the window, the atmosphere in the room changes. Slowly, Jeremy turns to look at me.

Suddenly, I know what's coming. I want to run from the room. I want to keep pretending.

"We need to talk," he says.

I wait a second, but when he says nothing more, my anger flares. I refuse to be the victim. I face him squarely, chin held high. "I think we should call off the wedding."

He stands perfectly still, not even a blink. He heard me. He's just pissed that I said it first. I'm about to call him on that when he drops so hard into the desk chair it almost tips over. Oh, thank you, God. He's stunned. He's devastated. He's going to tell me I must be crazy to say such a thing.

"All right," he says quietly.

What?

All right?

Oh God. Oh God. Oh, God, no.

Everything I've suspected is true.

"Right," he says. He stands and reaches for the jacket he'd just taken off. "I'll stay at Ethan's tonight. We'll … revise … everything tomorrow."

I'm mute. I can only watch him walk out the door and close it behind him. Shutting me out of his life. This can't be happening. Oh God. This is happening. He's not going to argue with me. He's not going to tell me that, no matter what, he loves me, that I mean more to him than his bachelor life here in London. He said "all right." It's fine with him if we don't get married, if he stays here, if he never sees me again. It's all right. It's great, in fact. He's gone to Ethan's with the news that the Handsome One is back, baby. Let the party begin.

I can't breathe. My vision blurs. Am I dying? I touch my face. It's wet. I'm not dying. I'm only crying.

Footsteps on the stairs. My heart leaps. The door opens.

"Chelsea?"

It's Mom.

I don't remember moving, but here I am sitting on the edge of the bed with her. I can't feel my body. I can't tell if time is passing. Mom is talking, but I can't understand what she's saying. Someone else is in the room. Someone is holding my hand. And then someone is holding a glass to my lips, and I drink. Gin! I gasp and choke and cough and cough, and I'm still crying. But now I can hear. Mom's voice. Laura's voice.

"What's going on? Why did Jeremy leave? Talk to us. Chelsea. Chelsea. Chelsea."

"The wedding's off." And now it's really true because I've said it out loud.

"That's not possible," Mom says.

"Did my idiot brother say that?" Laura asks. "That's ridiculous."

Mom shakes her head. "You must have misunderstood, sweetie."

"Yes. That's it," Laura says. "You misunderstood. Jeremy's mad about you. He would never cancel the wedding."

They're both trying to convince themselves as much as they are me.

"No, I did. I said we should call it off."

They both jump to their feet and face me. Now, I'm the villain. An insane one, judging by the looks on their faces.

My mom jerks my chin up to make me look her in the eye. "Why the hell would you do that, Chelsea?"

Her cussing infuriates me. I grab a shirt from my opened suitcase and rub my face dry. "It doesn't matter why. I said we should, and he said that's fine with him. End of story." Silly me. With my mom, there's no end to the story until she says so.

"What were you two arguing about before you said that?"

Laura lays a hand on her arm. "I don't think they were arguing, Marie. I think Chelsea expected Jeremy to call her bluff. Didn't you?"

I nod. "But that was stupid because I've known it was coming to this for a while."

My mom sinks down beside me again. "I don't understand. I thought you two were happy. I know you were. You bought your wedding dress just ten days ago. What happened to change that?"

I feel so heavy. I just want to lie down. I want to sleep and sleep and sleep. I look at Laura, sending a silent appeal. She gives me a tiny sad smile.

"Marie," she says, "I think Chelsea needs to be alone right now."

"Thank you," I say.

When my mom turns to leave, Laura slips a prescription bottle from her pocket and sets it on the nightstand. "I thought you might like a Xanax to take the edge off," she whispers, and then louder, "We'll be downstairs when you want to talk."

Just before the door clicks closed behind them, Laura says something about killing Jeremy.

I'm glad, now, that I didn't take the Xanax. My mind has been churning, and I've figured out what I need to do. But first, I have to see if the coast is clear. My mom is supposed to have a date with Jeremy's uncle tonight. She needs to go. Just because my life has turned to crap, it doesn't mean she should miss out on her second chance at love. I climb off the bed and go into the bathroom. A few minutes later, with my hair combed and my makeup repaired, I head downstairs.

My mom is alone in the kitchen. Her hands are curled around a full cup of tea that I'd bet has gone cold. The TV is on, and she's staring in that direction, but I know she's not watching it because it's tuned to a British political discussion, and she doesn't even pay much attention to American politics. She jumps when I speak.

"Oh, Chelsea, I didn't hear you come in."

She motions to the chair beside hers. I walk up to the table but don't sit down. "Where's Laura?"

My mom freezes, her eyes huge. "Um ... she had an errand to run."

Uh-huh, she's out killing Jeremy. Good. "Why aren't you getting ready to leave, Mom?"

"Leave?"

I fake a huge smile. "How could you forget you're going to dinner with Uncle Bert?"

"Oh." She looks around her. "My phone. I need to call him and cancel."

I spy her phone before she does and grab it. "Nope. You need to go, Mom. You are going."

"Not after ... what's happened."

I laugh. It's a little shaky but convincing enough. "You know I can be a drama queen, Mom. Jeremy and I will work it out. So you can't use that as an excuse to back out of tonight."

"I'm not backing out. Bert will understand. Now give me my phone."

"I think you're getting cold feet." I slip her phone in my jeans pocket.

"I am not."

"Then prove it. Go upstairs and start getting ready. Now."

She actually stands and walks out of the room. That was easier than I expected. I wait until her footsteps sound in the hall above before I start creeping up the stairs. When her bedroom door shuts, I run up to our room, dial for a taxi, and gather what little I'd already unpacked from the country stay. It will be easier for Jeremy and I to "revise everything" when there's five thousand miles between us. I have my suitcases inside the car waiting at the curb before I knock on my mom's door.

"Come in."

"Way to go, Mom. You look great."

She huffs. "I'm not even finished with my makeup."

"Okay, you will look great." I flash another fake smile. "Anyway, I came up to give you back your phone and to tell you that I'm going over to Ethan's to talk to Jeremy."

"Oh, Chelsea." She lays down her mascara wand and grabs me in a hug. "That's exactly what you should do. I know he's sorry about your fight and just afraid to make the first move. Men are weak."

"Yeah, I know. So if we're not back before you leave, have a wonderful time." God, I feel like such a jerk for lying to her. I kiss her cheek and hand her the phone. I'm down the stairs, out the door, and into the taxi before the tears start again. I'm a horrible daughter to make her travel back to LA alone, but I can't stay here four more days. I just can't.

A half hour later, as the driver is unloading my luggage to an airport cart, it occurs to me that changing my ticket to the next flight might not be so easy. I mean, when is the next flight? It's nearly six now. Oh, wait. There'll be a red-eye. I pay the driver and also tip the man standing beside the cart even though he didn't do much but hold it steady for the taxi driver. Oh, who cares? I won't need this British money after tonight anyway. I grab the cart—the trolley, as Jeremy would say—oh God. Don't think about him now. I push my luggage into the terminal and look for the shortest line of passengers. Is there one specifically for changing your flight? I ask a passing flight attendant, and she points me in the right direction.

Luckily, it's not a long line. Soon, I step up to the sweet-looking mom type behind the counter. "I need to change my ticket to an earlier flight."

"Certainly, luv. May I see your photo ID, please?"

I hand her my ticket along with my driver's license. She looks at both and types something. "Your flight is scheduled for 8:20 a.m. I'm afraid that is the earliest flight to New York on that day."

"I want to change the day of my flight too."

"And what day would that be, miss?"

"Today. Tonight."

She arches her brows and then smiles at me as if indulging a child. "All seats on our flights tonight are reserved."

"What about first class? Business class? I'll pay whatever."

Her patronizing smile grows. "I'm sure you would, dear. But we have none available."

"What about cancellations. Are you telling me not one single person has canceled?"

She turns her steely eyes back to the computer screen but doesn't type anything. "Yes. I'm sorry, but all seats are taken. Would you like me to check tomorrow's flights?"

Crap. "Yes. Please." If I have to spend the night in the airport, I will. Whatever. I can't believe it when she shakes her head. "You've got to be kidding."

"I assure you, I'm not."

She's lying to me. Never in the history of the world has there ever been an airport this huge, with this many flights, that had every single damn seat taken.

"Standby." That came out a little louder than I intended. I swear she looks down her nose at me. A considerable size nose at that.

"You needn't shout, ma'am."

And you needn't be such a pain in the ass. "You do have standby in this country, don't you?"

"We do. Would you like me to add your name to the standby list?"

"Crap. There's a list?"

"Always, ma'am."

I could get frostbite from her smile now. "Yes, add me to your stupid list."

She types something. My name, I presume, but she's acting like such a bitch, you never know.

"There you go. Now I need to see your passport, Miss Cole."

Oh fucking no. My passport is back at Laura's, in Jeremy's messenger bag.

"Miss Cole?"

"I don't have it."

Now she arches one brow and looks down her nose. "In that case, I can't help you."

"Yeah, and you're just fucking delighted about that, aren't you?"

I grab my ID and ticket and spin away from the counter, forgetting that my luggage cart is right behind me. There's no stopping my forward momentum. I flip over the cart and land flat on my back, the breath knocked out of me. I can't believe I'm sprawled on the floor, looking at the ceiling. When I can breathe, I start laughing. And crying. And sobbing. And full-on boohooing in the middle of the British Airways lobby of Heathrow Airport. What are the odds no one's watching?

I close my eyes and try to get myself under control. Two seconds later, I sense I have company and look up into the faces of two airport security guards.

"Is there a problem, miss?"

Ohmygod. British reserve is the funniest thing in the world. Is there a problem? I start laughing so hard I'm afraid I'll pee myself.

"Miss, are you hurt?"

There's an edge to Guard Number One's voice now. I choke back my laugh to a giggle and shake my head.

"Up you go, then." They grab my arms and lift me to my feet.

Guard Number Two leans in closer, sniffing. "Been having a tipple, eh?"

"No." Uh-oh, can he smell the gin? "Just one sip."

Guard Number Two presses his lips together with a hmm.

Guard Number One says, "Drugs?"

"No." Uh-oh, Laura's Xanax are in my purse. Ohmygod. I'm going to be busted. They'll jail me for possession of prescription drugs without a prescription. Or whatever. And her name is on the bottle—Laura Pearce—daughter of Judge Gordon Pearce. I'm ruining the family name. And I'm not even going to be part of the family anymore. Wait. Problem solved. I'll just say I stole them.

I look for my purse and see Guard Number Three, a woman, hanging it from my luggage cart. Then we're all moving away from the counter and at least a thousand staring passengers. I consider the odds of my grabbing the cart and outrunning them, but two of the guards look pretty fit, and they'd gladly leave the other one in the dust to nab this obviously insane American woman. There's no escape.

They lead me into a small room with a table and chairs, bright lights, and no windows. Here's where they'll tear through every inch of my luggage. And strip-search me. Don't forget that. That's why they called for the female guard. And who called them anyway? The steely-eyed bitch. Yep. Should have seen that coming.

Number Two leads me to a chair and orders me to sit. Number One sets a cup of water in front of me. And Number Three hands me a tissue. Oh, I get it. Two good cops and one bad one. Bring it on, Number Two. Let's get this over with.

Number Two takes the chair across from mine. He's holding my license and glances at it. "Is there someone we could call for you, Miss Cole?"

I'm suspicious because his tone is too kind. It must be a trick. "No. I just want to fly home."

"California must be lovely," he says. "My wife's always nattering on about going on holiday there."

So, I guess Number Two isn't the bad cop after all. The other two guards remain standing, one on either side of me. I'm on edge waiting for the screws to turn. When Number One sneezes, I flinch.

"Sorry," he says. "Allergies."

I risk a glance up at Number Three. Is she the one supposed to break me? She smiles. Sweetly. I'm confused.

"Forgive me for prying, Miss Cole," says Two, "but it appears you may have suffered a bad experience."

I stare at him. I'm not saying any more than I have to.

"With you wanting to cut short your trip, you see."

"Or possibly some emergency's come up at home?" says Three.

"Right," says One. He lays a hand on my shoulder. "Is that it, luv? An emergency?"

Are they serious? The door opens, and an airline employee hands Two a sheet of paper. He reads it and then looks at me.

"You're here with traveling companions? A Jeremy Pearce and Mrs. Marie Cole. Your mother?"

I give up, deflating with a sigh. "There's no emergency. And the bad experience here is personal. I just wanted to go home, but I forgot my passport back at … the hotel, and that … that woman out there wouldn't put me on the standby list, and I just lost it. I'm sorry. I caused a scene, and I know you guys hate that. I'm very, very sorry. But I didn't break any laws, did I?"

"Awww, luv." Three squats beside my chair. "Could I get you a nice cup of tea?"

This is surreal. "Um … sure?"

"Biscuits would be nice," says One as he and Three scurry out the door.

Two smiles at me. "No, Miss Cole, you didn't break any laws. We're just here to help. And to give you a chance to collect yourself."

"Thank you." I imagine my makeup is a mess again, but I'm not going to ask for my purse and give him a chance to see that pill bottle. No sense rocking the boat here. I wipe my eyes with the tissue, hoping I'm not making my face look worse.

"Would you like to visit the toilet?"

I hesitate before nodding. Will he have to go in with me? He stands. I hold my breath.

"It's just out the door and to your left."

"Thanks." When I start toward the door, he sits. Okay, then. Of course, he probably figures I'm not likely to run off without my luggage. But what if I ask for my purse? I step to the cart and lift the strap. "Can I take this with me?"

He blushes. "Certainly."

Just as I enter the restroom, I realize why he was embarrassed. He probably thought I needed a tampon from my purse. I pee, wash my hands, and fix my face a bit. Dropping the pill bottle in the trash can as I exit takes a big weight off.

One and Three have returned. "We're taking our break with you," says Three.

So here I am, sitting in a private room in Heathrow Airport having tea and cookies with three airport cops. Yep, surreal.

After our tea, Guards One, Two, and Three wish me well and direct me to the exit near the taxi stand. I've told them I'm going back to the hotel. I wheel my cart out the exit, in case they're watching, and then walk toward the first taxi in line. But I don't get in. I move back against the wall and stand with my luggage. It's after nine, and I'm exhausted.

I need Gabi. I dial her number, calmer already because I know she'll see this clearly from the outside and tell me what to do, but it rings until her voicemail comes on. Crap. What am I going to do now?

Think, Chelsea, think.

I can't leave the country without my passport. I can't get

my passport unless I go back to Laura's. Can I count on her still being out looking for Jeremy? Could I keep the taxi waiting, run upstairs, grab my passport, and come back here without anyone being the wiser? It's worth a try.

Oh crap. I don't have a key.

I get in a taxi anyway. Where else am I going to go but back to Laura's? Hey, what if I went in the back gate? I'm sure I can find some way inside. The image of Bridget Jones climbing onto her boyfriend's skylight comes to mind. But I need to get inside not just look. Hmm.

thirteen

Laura's car is parked on the street. Well, that's that. I pay the taxi driver and wrangle my suitcases up to the door. The door's locked, of course, so I have to ring the bell. Laura answers, her surprise deepening as she looks from me to my luggage and back.

"Don't ask," I say.

"How can I not? You were leaving without telling any-one?"

"No. Yes." Sigh. "I told you not to ask."

She shakes her head in reproof but helps me get my stuff inside. I grab the largest case and start up the stairs.

"Leave it," she orders. "You owe me an explanation."

She heads toward the living room, and I set the bag down and follow. What choice do I have?

There's a half-full glass and an open bottle of wine on the coffee table. She turns off the TV, picks up the glass, and tucks a foot under her as she drops onto the sofa.

"Get a glass and come sit, Chelsea."

She waits until I take a couple of sips before she speaks again.

"Jeremy is at Ethan's."

I nod.

"He wouldn't talk to me."

That surprises me. They're so close. She's waiting for me to say something, but what can I?

She sighs. "He's not talking to Ethan either."

"So … what is he doing?"

"Crying."

"Crying!" I've never seen Jeremy cry.

"Not outwardly, of course. He was brought up as a god-damned Pearce, after all."

Laura tears up but instantly swallows her emotion, just like I've seen Jeremy do. She picks up a throw pillow and, with an angry whimper, launches it across the room. Then she drains her glass, gets up, and stomps to the bar.

"We're going to need another bottle," she says. "Maybe two." After she's seated again, her eyes widen, and she slaps her thigh. "I've forgotten where your mother is. I thought she might be with you."

"She's out with your uncle."

Laura points a finger at me and nods. I suspect she may have already killed a bottle on her own tonight.

"I'm sorry this has upset you, Laura, but—"

"Upset?" She rises from the sofa corner she'd slumped into. "Upset, you say? It kills me to see my brother dying inside."

God, I feel like crap. I should have kept my mouth shut. I should have let Jeremy call off the wedding and—hey, wait. This is all wrong. If anyone has the right to die inside, it's me.

"I don't know why Jeremy should be upset," I say. "He's the one who's getting what he wants."

Laura stares at me, swaying a bit. She props herself up against the sofa arm, and then gestures for me to refill her glass. I fill both of ours nearly to the brims. To hell with giving it room to breathe.

"That makes no sense." She frowns and, for a moment, transfers her stare to the wine in her glass. "Didn't you say you broke the engagement?"

"Yes, but only because he was getting ready to do it."

"No. Uh-uh. I don't believe he was. He wouldn't be in the state he's in now if that were true."

I set my glass down and take Laura's from her. "Look around you, Laura. Think of your parents' homes. And the cars, and the clubs, and all that … society. That's what Jeremy would be giving up. And I've seen him with you and his friends here. He's a totally different person from the Jeremy I know. And this city, that alone—"

"You're completely mental." She sits forward, suddenly sobered, eyes blazing. "You apparently don't know Jeremy at all if you think those things mean more to him than you do."

I'm on my feet in an instant. "Are you blind? You've been with us almost every minute we've been in London. Haven't you noticed how quiet he's gotten? How depressed?"

She's shaking her head like I don't know what I'm talking about. "He and Dad—"

"It's not just because of his problems with your dad."

She's still shaking her head.

"We haven't had sex in three days, Laura."

There. That got through to her. I sit back down. She stands.

"I need coffee."

I follow her to the kitchen. I need coffee too. This is going to be a long night.

We don't speak again until our cappuccinos are ready. Laura hands me one, and we take chairs on opposite sides of the table. There's a huge skylight over this part of the kitchen. I look up at the moon. How did this trip turn out so horrible?

"So," Laura says, "tell me word for word how the conversation with Jeremy went." When I'm done reciting how I remember it, she says, "Did it occur to you that he might not have expected you to say what you did?"

Sigh. "I told you he's been working up to saying the same thing for days."

She looks into her cup for a moment. "But you say he collapsed into the chair."

"Yeah. With relief."

"Not shock?"

"No ..."

"And then he said ..."

"All right. He just said 'all right,' and then he walked out."

"Did he sound relieved when he said that?"

"No. Well ... not exactly. He sounded like Jeremy. Like ... like when he's ..."

"When he's trying to hide his real feelings?"

Oh, God.

"I saw him when he left, Chelsea. The look on his face wasn't relief. And it certainly wasn't joy."

"Oh, God."

"Yes. That bad."

"But ... but then if it wasn't that he'd changed his mind about our getting married, why has he been acting so unhappy with me these last few days?"

She stands. "I don't know, but we're off to Ethan's to find out."

Ethan answers the door with a beer in hand. "Thank God you've come. I was beginning to think I'd have to resort to torture to make him talk."

I'm still not positive Laura's right that I misinterpreted the situation, but something's definitely wrong if Jeremy won't even tell Ethan what's going on. A soccer game is on TV, but apparently only Ethan was watching it. Jeremy is sitting next to a window, looking out at the city lights, and doesn't turn his head toward us when we walk into the room. His hair hangs loose on his shoulders. Somehow he seems smaller. Laura's right: he looks like he's crying inside. The first time I saw him flashes back to me, how lonely he looked. It sounds cliché, but I really do think my heart is bleeding. How can I live without this man in my life?

Ethan, not bothering with playing host, returns to the sofa. Laura and I exchange a look. I stay by the door, and she goes to Jeremy.

"Jemmy, will you talk to me now?"

His only response is to turn his head farther away from her.

She bites her lip. For a moment, she stares out the window with him. Then she sighs. "Jeremy, why did Chelsea think you'd changed your mind about marriage?"

As if Laura's words are on time delay, a few seconds pass before he looks at her. Bewilderment is written all over his face. My hopes rise before they're smacked down by the thought that maybe he didn't hear her actual words.

She crouches to be eye level with him and takes hold of

one of his hands. "She believes you no longer want to marry her."

The real Jeremy awakes with a bang. "That's preposterous!"

Laura stands upright and beckons me with a look. When Jeremy follows her gaze, his face registers a second of surprise before confusion warps it. I'm barely breathing as I start across the room. If I was wrong, I've hurt him terribly. How can I apologize for that? He stands when I'm about eight feet from him, and I stop dead. A bazillion emotions are spinning in my head, and when the wheel stops on anger, I explode.

"Preposterous? Then why did you agree so quickly?"

He rears back. "You expected me to argue with your decision? Beg you to marry me even though you clearly don't want to?"

His righteous indignation is evident, but I know him well enough to see it's only about eighty percent genuine. "Don't deny you've had doubts now that—"

"Naturally, I have fleeting moments of doubt, like any man would do."

"But you've had serious doubts since we've been in London."

He narrows his eyes in true Mr. High Tea fashion, which means I've struck a nerve. I'm not going to let that go. If we can't be honest with our feelings, then our marriage will be doomed anyway.

"Well?"

He straightens his back to stand as tall as possible, looming his six-foot-three over my five-foot-four. I'm positive, now, that he can't deny having second thoughts. But dare I hope that, in the last few hours, he's had third thoughts?

"I am never going to be wealthy," he says.

"If you marry me, you mean?"

Okay, it looks like I've bewildered him again, and I have no idea how. Finally, he shakes his head.

"You've confused the point," he says. "I will never be wealthy, and that's why I can't marry you."

I know it's hard to believe, but I'm speechless. For thirty seconds. "Are you saying my mother demanded some exorbitant bride price from you?"

Absolute silence fills the room for ten seconds before Laura and Ethan snicker and then burst out laughing. Jeremy's not laughing or even smiling. He's clearly questioning my sanity.

"Stop it," I tell Laura and Ethan. As they're murmuring apologies, I turn back to Jeremy. "Obviously, I don't know what you meant. I've already downsized the wedding plans, and my mother's paying for most of that anyway. So you can't use money as an excuse not to marry me."

Oh great, now he's looking at me like I've "gone mental." He steps over to the sofa and picks up his jacket. Then he grabs my hand and starts pulling me toward the door.

"Where are you going?" Laura asks.

"For a walk. Chelsea and I need to talk."

"Thank God," Ethan says.

It's freezing outside, and I'm wearing only a light jacket. I hope this walk doesn't take too long, but I'm not going to complain—or say anything until Jeremy does. We're halfway down the street before he speaks.

"We're not communicating well."

"Ya think?"

He stops walking and faces me. Damn my snarky mouth. I start to apologize, but then he shakes his head, smiling.

"Bride price?" he says. "Seriously?"

"Don't make fun of me. Explain what you meant about being wealthy."

We start off down the street again. I cross my arms and tuck my hands in my armpits. There's a pub up ahead, and I hope that's where we're headed. He can't expect me to have a sensible conversation with a half-frozen brain.

"First," he says, "I think you should explain why you canceled our wedding. Not even postponed. Just quashed the possibility."

"I said that because I thought you were about to do it."

He stops again and gapes at me. "Setting aside, for the moment, that you had no cause to believe such a thing, it's disturbing that you would choose to blurt out that shocking pronouncement as an exercise in one-upmanship."

"I know. I'm sorry." I start walking; he keeps pace.

"Right. Well then, why did you think I was about to say the same thing?"

"You haven't been yourself for the last few days. And nights. What else was I supposed to think?"

He pulls his hair back into a tail but let's it fall loose again when he realizes he has nothing to bind it with. "So to you us not having sex means … all right, yes. I've not been myself. But not because I wanted to end our relationship."

I'm losing the feeling in my fingers and toes, and we've reached the pub. "Could we go in there?"

"Oh. Yes, of course."

The pub is warm and small but not too crowded. I find a table in a corner, and he brings us pints. As he lifts the glass to his lips, he motions for me to continue our talk. I'm trying to remember where we left off when he prompts me.

"Why, besides the lack of sex, did you think I'd changed my mind?"

"You seemed depressed. It's obvious how much you miss living here, so I knew you were adding up what marrying me would cost you and decided—"

"Dear God. How many times have you promised to stop jumping to conclusions?"

"I didn't jump. I thought about it for days. I tried very hard to convince myself I was wrong."

"Well, you didn't try hard enough."

"Don't be an ass. I was devastated. Totally destroyed."

He makes that irritating head-exploding gesture that he damn well knows I can't stand, and then he leans across the table to get in my face.

"I was not counting the costs of marrying you because there are none. No losses. Only benefits."

"Liar. I see how you miss your life here. How you are with your friends—happy, relaxed, the life of the party."

He sits back in his chair, shaking his head and looking at the ceiling as though he can't believe what he just heard. Enough. This "talk" is going nowhere. I stand and start to walk out but turn back to drain my glass—no use wasting an excellent beer—and then I head for the door. I don't get far down the street before I hear him running up behind me.

"Chelsea."

I ignore him. He grabs me around the waist and lifts me so my feet are dangling.

"Let go of me."

"Not until you promise to calm down and have a proper conversation."

I kick him in the shins, and he drops me.

"I was having a proper conversation. And you were mocking me, you jerk." My breathing hitches. No, no, no. Don't you dare cry, Chelsea Cole. I don't even see Jeremy move, but suddenly he's kissing me. And then I'm kissing him back. This has got to be the most confusing night of my life. Ever.

"I'll hail a taxi," he says when we take a breath. "Let's go back to Laura's."

A few minutes later, I'm snuggled up to Jeremy in the taxi. I know we haven't settled everything, but I don't care. I just want to get him into bed. And then sleep. Tomorrow is soon enough to sort out all the misunderstandings. He sees only benefits in marrying me. I can't ask for more than that.

When we arrive at Laura's, I wait by the door while he pays the driver. It's just occurred to me he might not have a key on him, when he steps up and slips one in the lock. As he swings open the door, I remember what's sitting in the entrance.

Oh. My. God.

Laura left the light on in the entry hall, so when Jeremy steps in, he freezes. The pause before he speaks is a giant hand squeezing my heart.

"What's this?"

"It's … my luggage."

The look he gives me asks how I could be so insensitive to state the obvious in a moment like this. I wish I could come up with a believable lie to save this night from a horrible end, but the truth is right there in front of us.

"I was running away."

"And Laura stopped you?"

Here's where I could salvage the situation—possibly. I

could secretly text Laura to go along with the lie, and I'm pretty sure she would.

"No. I got to the airport and didn't have my passport, so I had to come back. I'm sorry. I was freaked out and hurt and thinking crazy."

Jeremy says nothing. He's looking at me, but his eyes are doing that faraway thinking thing. After what seems like an hour, he shoulders one bag, lifts the largest one, and starts up the stairs. I'm so relieved, I have to catch my breath before I can grab the rest and follow.

When I enter our room, he takes the bags I'm carrying, tosses them to the floor, and kicks the door closed.

"Three nights," he mutters, and then he's kissing me and undressing me at the same time.

When he picks me up to lay me on the bed, I choke up. This. This feeling of being safe in his arms is what I never want to be without. He's my protector. My lover. My man. Even now in his desire to make up for three lost nights, he kisses me gently, moving slowly.

"No," I tell him, "I want you inside me now. Now." I reach for him, guiding him. I'm desperate for him. "Make me scream. Make me lose my mind." I claw at his back.

"No, wait. No."

"Yes. Yesss." I wrap my legs around him tighter. He's my captive. My slave. "Do it."

I'm delirious with wanting him. We're delirious together. And then everything explodes at once. It's heaven.

"Oh my God, woman," he says when he collapses beside me. "That was insane. Who are you?"

"Hold me," I say, snuggling up to him.

"I'll do anything you say."

"Maybe we should take a hiatus more often."

"If you do that to me every time after, I don't think my heart will last long."

I laugh, but a second later, I'm crying.

"No, no, please don't." He squeezes me tighter. "I'm sorry. I love you. We're fine now. Aren't we?"

Now I'm laughing again. He tilts my face up toward his. He looks so bewildered it makes me laugh harder. He sits us up and grasps me by my shoulders.

"Chelsea, are you all right? Should I call your mother?"

That question sobers me pronto. "I need to pee."

He's still sitting up when I come out of the bathroom. "Are you sure you're all right?"

"No. I'm not."

He looks crushed. "What can I do?"

I climb on the bed and straddle him. "You can kiss me."

He smiles. "Is that all?"

"Not by a mile."

Later, when I'm satiated again and on the edge of sleep, my brain echoes something Jeremy said at Ethan's: "I will never be wealthy, and that's why I can't marry you." I sit up. He never explained what he meant by that.

"Jeremy?" He doesn't respond, so I push his shoulder.

"What? What?"

"Why do you need to be rich to marry me?"

He groans. "Misunderstanding."

"Yeah, I don't understand, so explain."

"Sleep. Leave it till morning."

He rolls to his side and pulls the covers over his head. Like that's going to end this conversation. I'm thinking back to his "all right" reaction. He may not have been happy about my decision, but still. Something doesn't add up ... unless. I was right! I shove him. Hard.

"You were going to call off our wedding."

He groans again.

"Get your ass up, Jeremy. You're not sleeping until you explain yourself."

He sits up with a huge drama-queen sigh. "Why must you beat a dead horse?"

"This horse isn't dead."

He opens his mouth, shuts it, and then rubs his face hard. "I want to marry you. You want to marry me. So why can't we leave it at that?"

"Because you haven't told me why you—"

"You want more than I can give you." He glances at me, then leans back against the headboard and closes his eyes.

I don't know what he means. Or maybe I do and can't face it, but if he's saying what I think he's saying, why would he change his mind and marry me anyway? I feel sick.

"Why would you marry me if you don't love me?"

For the hundredth time tonight, he looks at me as if I'm totally out of my mind.

"If you can harbor any doubt that I love you, you are mental." He puts his arm around my shoulders and pulls me close. "Love is what I can give you. It's the other things I can't. I've watched your reactions to everything here. To Dovewood House especially. I was hoping you'd find the Pearce family lifestyle a bore, actually. But you didn't. You'd love having two houses and six cars and a busy social life and —"

"Holy shit." I'm slapping his chest while he leans away as far as he can without falling sideways off the bed. "You frigging hypocrite."

"What the hell are you on about now?"

"I'm the one who jumps to conclusions? What do you call

thinking I'm so shallow that after I saw Dovewood I wanted to dump you and find some rich guy to marry?"

"Well … but … I—"

"Of course, there is Richard …"

"Don't even."

I pull him back to cuddle. "Actually, it's kind of funny that you thought I wanted the exact things I thought you were sorry you'd given up."

"I'm not sorry. I told you there are no losses—"

"Okay, but could you get them back?"

"You mean, could I give up writing, go back to the family's law firm, and kiss my father's arse for the rest of my life?"

"Yes. Could you?"

"Yes. I could do." He slides down to lie flat on the bed, pulling me with him. "But would I? No." He kisses my nose. "No." He kisses my lips. "Never." He kisses my neck. "Not if it meant giving you up."

"But what if you could have the money and me too? I mean, that country house is hella mind-blowing, and that Rolls …"

He interrupts his trail of kisses down my body to study my face. I struggle to keep a giggle in, but it escapes.

"You are a cruel, absolutely heartless woman, Chelsea Cole." He moves back up on the bed and raises himself on one elbow. "I'm crazy about you. Will you marry me?"

"Hmm. I think I need to see how you rate in the sex department before I can answer that."

"Ah. Then get out your tally sheet, woman."

fourteen

We leave for home in sixty-six hours. Jeremy and I are walking back to Laura's. She had to go into work for a couple of hours today, and Mom's out with Uncle Bert, so it was just the two of us for lunch. Ethan's invited us to a party at his place tomorrow night, which means Laura, Jeremy, and I will be wiped out for half of Saturday, and then Uncle Bert and Mom are taking us out for the evening. I'm cool with those plans. What I'm nervous about is tonight's dinner with Gordon and Amanda.

"So," I say as we're crossing Portobello Road, "we're going to be open and honest from now on, right?"

"Yes."

"With everyone?"

"Well … define open and honest. Define everyone. I mean, there are instances where—"

"I'm talking about your parents. About me. My look. The real me."

"Oh. In that case, yes. Which, if you recall, is how I wanted you to be from the start."

"Yeah, yeah. So I need to find a salon and do a little shopping."

He stops on the corner and pulls out his phone. "Laura and I favored the same salon. I'll get you in."

Two minutes later, he's booked me for an "emergency" color and styling. A last-minute appointment. On a Friday. Boy does money talk.

"Now, your clothes." He looks up the street. "This way, I think."

The first shop Jeremy pulls me into has fabulous real vintage clothes—with prices to match—and I nix that one. In another shop, we find a supercute print dress. The background is black with fantasy butterflies in jewel tones, which sounds dopey, but it's not. Jeremy declares it "smashing." But it's sleeveless, so we go in search of a light jacket. I'm just about to give up when we turn a corner and find the dream shop. I gather an armful of possibles and head to the dressing room. To get the full effect, I put on the dress. The third jacket I try is a hit. It's a silk bolero, purple, red, and black plaid. (It works. Believe me.)

"Shoes?" Jeremy asks when we're walking down the street again.

"I don't know. Maybe I'll save the money and wear my black pumps or borrow a pair of boots from Laura. With black tights, it—" I shut my mouth because I see what Jeremy's pointing to. The coolest stiletto ankle boots I've ever seen. They're purple suede with a fringed cuff. Adorable.

Jeremy's already ushering me in the door.

We don't finish at the salon until well into teatime, so Jeremy and I stop in a crowded pub for one drink and a nibble. I try not to notice the looks I'm getting. I wonder what they're making of the contradiction between my conservative clothes and funky hair.

"Do you feel like yourself again?" Jeremy asks as he pulls out my chair.

"Yes, but I'm worried about how your parents will react."

"Right. Without their approval, I'll have no choice but to call off the wedding."

"Point taken, smart-ass."

"So there's nothing to worry about, is there?"

"Yes. There is. You don't care what they think of me, but I do. And now they're going to meet the real me."

Jeremy sighs and goes to the bar to get our drinks and order our starter. Some guy comes up and slaps him on the back. They talk until our pints are ready. I notice how many women give Jeremy the eye as he walks toward me. He looks only at me. I can't believe we broke each other's hearts only a few days ago.

Jeremy sits down. "You are the most beautiful woman here."

"Which means you've looked at them all?"

"No need to."

He takes a drink and then takes my hand. "Where were we? Oh, yes. Except for the way you looked, do you actually think you hid the real Chelsea from my parents?"

"Ohmygod. What did I do wrong? Why didn't you tell me I was embarrassing you? Or insulting them?" His eyebrows have risen higher with each question.

"Conclusion jumping, love. You did nothing wrong. Even the outburst at lunch on Monday was my fault, not yours. You charmed them."

"They told you that?" The wait for his answer while the appetizer is set before us is agonizing.

"They offered to hold our wedding at their home, and when we declined that, they lobbied for a second wedding reception."

"Well, that's just because you're their son."

He shakes his head like he can't believe I said that and pops a pakora in his mouth. His eyes bulge and start watering. I try but can't hold in a laugh as he struggles with how to stop the burning. Finally, he thinks to take a gulp of his beer.

"Thanks for the sympathy," he says.

"I would have spit it out."

"Yes, you would have."

"And you would have been mortified."

He looks past me for a second, considering, and then shakes his head. "Once I would have ... but not any longer."

"That's the most loving thing you've ever said to me."

He cocks his right eyebrow. "I've clearly been wasting a lot of effort."

"We're going to love each other for the rest of our lives, aren't we?"

He grimaces. "For that long?"

I smack his arm. He jumps up, pulls me into his arms, and kisses me right in front of everyone. Then he looks me in the eye. "Even death won't stop me."

I try to play it off, but tears sting my eyes. I can't believe it when he stands back and sweeps an arm toward me, announcing, "My angel and fiancée."

"You've lost your mind," I say amid the cheers.

He shrugs. "Let's go. I need to shower again before dinner. Since we're being real tonight, I think I'll leave my hair down."

That's my man, willing to go down in flames with me.

"In here," Laura calls out to us when we walk in the door. She and Mom are having a gin and tonic. I hide behind Jeremy until we're in the living room, and then I pop out.

My mom's mouth drops open when she sees my hair. Laura laughs. "Now that's the way to liven up a Pearce family dinner."

"Hush, Laura." Jeremy walks toward the bar. "I've just talked her out of being stressed."

"Maybe you should have waited to change your hair," Mom says.

"Hell no," Laura says. "It's about time she showed her true colors."

"Ha. No pun intended?" Jeremy says. "I never wanted her to hide them in the first place."

"And you shouldn't have," Laura says to me. "You're on trend. Bomb ass."

Jeremy gives me a thumbs-up. "Wait till you see her out-fit."

"Oh my." Mom gulps her drink.

"Geez, Mom, you're not helping."

Jeremy hands me a Batiste. "Drink this before you have a panic attack."

"Are you serious?" Laura says. "Do I need to slap you, girl? You're the bold one. The one who doesn't give a fuck what others think."

"I am?"

"Well, you were when I first met you."

Oh yeah. I was. I throw back my drink. "Okay. This is me. Love me or leave me."

Jeremy grins and pulls me toward the hall. "We'll see you in a bit."

When I come out of the bathroom, ready to go to dinner, Jeremy's pulling on his boots. I stop dead. He's wearing black jeans and one of his highland shirts—the kind that made me think he was some kind of poet when I first saw him. His gorgeous hair hangs a few inches past his shoulders, but he usually pulls it into a tail before he goes out.

"Are you really going to leave your hair down?"

"I am."

"And you're wearing those clothes?"

"You don't approve?"

"You know I do, but your—" He cocks that damn brow at me. "Okay. You're right. We're being ourselves."

He stands and pulls me to his side before the full-length mirror. "What do you think?"

"I think we're fabulous. And formidable. The hottest couple in two countries."

"Only two?"

I go to the closet and pull out his black leather racer jacket. "You need to wear this."

"Too right."

Mom's tightened lips when she sees both of us being ourselves says she's still worried about the Pearces' reaction. But her lips curve into a half smile when Laura applauds us.

Ten minutes later, we're walking into the Pearce's townhouse. I assume we'll start with drinks, like we did last time, before going up to the drawing room, but Laura ushers us toward the stairs. I hold Jeremy back. "Can we have a drink down here first?"

"Laura." He motions her toward the parlor or whatever they call the little room off the entry hall. Mom sighs with relief. Jeremy walks straight to the bar and mixes our usuals—our London usuals, that is.

Laura taps her foot as she sips. "Why are you so anxious for us to go upstairs?" I ask her.

"It's been a long time coming."

"What has?" my mom asks.

Grinning, Laura points to Jeremy. He gives her a steady look that says he's not clueless, but he's also not sure he agrees.

"I don't get what's going on," I say.

Laura swallows the last of her drink and stands. "You're what's going on, Chelsea. Come on. Drink up and let's go."

At the top of the stairs, Laura grabs my mom's hand and rushes through the door to be greeted instantly. Ten seconds later, Jeremy and I enter. The room goes dead silent. Surprise propels Gordon to his feet. He casts a frown at Jeremy and then fixes his gaze on me.

"Your hair is … gray … and purple," he says.

"It's silver," Amanda says, ignoring the look Gordon gives her. "And I love it. You look beautiful, Chelsea." Her gaze travels over both of us twice. "Quite handsome, Jeremy. And don't the two of you look perfect together?" Gordon stares at her like she's some crazy woman who's wandered into his house. "Breathe, Gordon," she says without looking at him.

"I do like your style," Uncle Bert says. "Smashing."

Gordon sinks back down into his chair.

"Cool jacket, Jeremy," Richard says.

Jeremy pauses, and I know he's waiting for the barb he expects to follow. I squeeze his hand, hoping to remind him of the conversation I had with Richard at the end of our Dovewood visit.

"Thank you, Richard," he says. "You should buy yourself one."

We drink and chitchat until dinner's announced. And then the discussion turns to the wedding and the two receptions. (Jeremy's accepted that we'll be returning here in June for the second.)

We've just been served the main course when Gordon looks at Jeremy. "Will you be cutting your hair before the wedding?"

"No."

Gordon sighs, looking so defeated I feel sorry for him. For a moment, he stares at his plate, and then he looks up hopefully. "Shave the beard?"

Jeremy glances at me. We've already discussed this. "Yes," he says and smiles.

Gordon smiles back. "Good. That's good."

A few minutes later, Richard speaks to Jeremy. "Are you ever going to write that literary novel?"

Jeremy looks at him blankly.

"You know, the one about the guy who volunteers to aid in Haiti after an earthquake and finds—"

"How do you know about that?" Jeremy barks.

"You told me. That night we got … uh"—he gives Gordon a nervous glance—"the night we smoked together?"

Jeremy's mouth opens, but then he just stares at Richard.

After a moment, Richard says, "Did I remember the story wrong?"

Jeremy gives a quick shake of his head as if to wake himself. "I've … forgotten that conversation. But, yes, that was an idea I had. Have, actually."

"Are you writing that book?" Gordon says.

"I said nothing," Amanda says when Jeremy looks to her.

Now we're all waiting for his answer.

"Yes," he says to Gordon. "I am."

It's my turn to gape. Jeremy's sudden interest in his napkin placement proves he's avoiding my eye.

Gordon nods. "That's a book I'll read."

Jeremy looks up at him, eyes wide. "Thank you."

I keep my mouth shut about Jeremy's literary novel through dessert and coffee, but after we say goodbye and get back in Laura's car, I let go. "How is it that your mother knew you're writing something I've never heard of? Did *you* know, Laura?" Her eyes give her away. "So your mother *and* your sister knew." I look behind me again. "Mom?"

"He mentioned it," she says quietly.

"What the fuck, Jeremy."

He gets out of the car. After a moment, I realize he's not getting back in, and I get out too. "What are you doing?"

"Waiting for you to cool down."

"I shouldn't have to cool down. I shouldn't have a reason to be upset."

We glare at each other over the roof of the car.

He looks away first. "I didn't know if I could do it."

"What does that have to do with telling everyone but me?"

He glances at me before dropping his gaze. We stand there under the streetlight, a cold wind tearing down the street and straight up my skirt.

"Jeremy?"

He still doesn't look up. "I didn't want you to know if I failed."

"But you haven't failed, have you?"

"I don't think so."

"I could have told you that you wouldn't fail. I know you. I recognize your talent. I believe in you."

He looks at me for a long time, swallowing hard, but the streetlights catch the glimmer in his eyes.

"Are we going to stand out here until I freeze solid?" I ask.

"I'm sorry … not for the cold … well, I mean—"

"Yeah, yeah. And what about Penny James?"

"She's all you now!" Laura yells from inside the car.

I look through the window at her and then at Jeremy.

"Me? Write by myself? I can't do that."

"Yes, you can," the three of them chorus.

I shake my head.

Jeremy walks around the car and puts his hands on my shoulders. "I know you. I recognize your talent. I believe in you."

♥ ♥ ♥

We've been at Ethan's party for an hour. I'm cold because the terrace doors are open, supposedly to clear some of the smoke, but still there's a thick haze adding a touch of unreality to the scene. At the moment, I'm standing where I can watch Ethan. And Ethan's watching Laura while pretending not to.

The thing about Ethan is that he thinks he hides his heart better than he does. Or is it just me that sees he's been in love with Laura for a long time? The saddest part is that he knows nothing can ever come of it. In Laura's eyes, Ethan's just another of her brothers. In Jeremy's eyes, though a great best friend, Ethan's also a womanizing dog he wouldn't allow within a mile of his sister.

Ethan catches me watching him and crosses the room to stand by me. "Why are you hiding back here? Not enjoying my party?"

"I'm just observing."

"Gathering material for your next book?"

"Not unless I'm going to write a sad story of unrequited love."

He looks me in the eye for a minute. "You're too observant I think."

"Possibly." I kiss his cheek. "I'm sorry."

"Life has a cruel sense of humor."

"Still …"

He nods. "Change the subject."

"Okay," I say. "So point out which of these women Jeremy's slept with."

"Ha." He takes a sip of his drink. "I'd prefer not to die at the hands of my best friend, if you don't mind."

"So some of them are here."

"I didn't say that."

"Yes, you did." I'm teasing, but my smile dies when then Ethan turns a serious face to me.

"None of that matters now."

"Oh, sure. I was only—"

"He loves you to a depth I never really believed possible." When a couple of loud guys join a woman near us, Ethan leads us a few feet away. "You already know he never intended to marry Alison, but the truth is, he never intended to marry anyone. We discussed it over many hours—some of them sober actually." Now he gives me that charming Ethan grin. "Can't say either of us saw anything but liabilities to marriage. Until he fell for you. And even then, I thought he'd get over it. Come to his senses." He looks across the room to where Jeremy's in conversation. "I've never been more wrong in my life." He turns back to me. "And I'm happy to say that."

"Thank you, Ethan."

He holds up his right hand and then leans close to my ear. "Just know that if you mess him up, I swear to get revenge. And I know where you live."

I'm speechless.

Ethan backs up, grinning. I smack his shoulder. He laughs, wraps an arm around me, and walks us toward the bar. "You're not drinking enough, luv."

♥ ♥ ♥

We're riding in Uncle Bert's Rolls on the way to dinner. Mom's spent so much time with him that I can't believe she's not acting sad about leaving London tomorrow. But maybe enjoying his company has opened her to dating more back home, and she's just looking forward to that.

Our reservations are at Duck & Waffle, which Jeremy assures me is a fantastic restaurant on the fortieth floor of a tower with a spectacular view of the city. I'm wearing the conservative black sheath dress I borrowed from Gabi, but spiced I've up with my new silk jacket and spike-heeled knee boots from Laura's closet.

Okay. So when Jeremy described the restaurant in a tower, I pictured some normal skyscraper. That's not what I see.

"It looks like a rocket," Mom says.

"It's nicknamed The Gherkin," Uncle Bert tells her.

"It looks like something else to me," I say.

"Chelsea!" Mom says, scandalized, but apparently oblivious that she's revealing she had the same thought.

Jeremy and Uncle Bert crack up.

A few minutes later, we're seated at a table with the London nightscape stretched before us. Wow. I'm trying not to overreact and make Jeremy insecure again, but geez. Being rich sure does have some benefits.

When the hostess produces the wine list, Uncle Bert looks to Jeremy. "Shall I?"

"By all means."

We sit for a few minutes, just sipping wine and looking at the view. Mom and Uncle Bert are talking quietly about something. I'm soaking up the experience. London has been an amazing adventure. Although it almost tore us apart, we've ended up closer than ever. I needed to see Jeremy here to fully understand and appreciate him.

"Thank you," he whispers to me.

"For what?"

"Everything, but especially for making me come back here. For giving me back my family."

"Even Richard?"

"We'll see," he says, but he's smiling.

The appetizers Uncle Bert ordered arrive, and we all try a bit of each. I'm open to anything tonight, so I let Jeremy order the entrée for me. Rabbit something.

It strikes me that Mom's gotten more adventurous here too. Or maybe she always was, and I just never noticed. I must be growing up.

Wine flows with each course. Everything is delicious. We're waiting for dessert when I realize Mom and Uncle Bert have leaned closer together and are smiling at us. Mom glances at him, and he nods.

"Well," she says and closes her eyes for a second, "Chelsea …" She grabs her wine glass and drains the last ounce.

"Ohmygod, Mom, what is it?"

"Albert and I are getting married."

I'm speechless—for a second. "But you just met. I mean, no offense, Uncle Bert, I think you're awesome. But, Mom, don't you think it's a little soon to make a decision like this?" Jeremy lays his hand on my thigh. I turn on him. "Did you know about this?"

"No."

"Chelsea," Mom says, "you tell me all the time I should have a life of my own."

"Yeah, but marriage—"

"Is what adults choose when they find someone they love and want to spend their life with."

"Yes, but … you don't really know each other. You can't love each other already."

"Yes, they can," Jeremy says.

I push his hand off my leg. "This doesn't concern you."

"Seriously?"

"Don't say that. You don't get to use that word anymore."

He sits back and looks at the ceiling.

"We didn't intend to upset you, Chelsea," Uncle Bert says.

"We thought you'd be happy for us, sweetie."

Jeremy pours more wine in my glass, and I down it. No one speaks. I've ruined this night. Jeremy fills my glass again. I look at him. He's got that damned right brow arched, and his eyes are saying plenty. He was right; Mom was keeping me close because she's lonely. She's been a widow for almost four years now. And even though I tried, I can't deny I saw the instant chemistry between her and Uncle Bert. I'm acting like a selfish brat.

Etiquette be damned; I gulp the wine. Then I take a breath, exhale, and face them.

"I'm sorry. Both of you. I am happy for you. I want you to be happy together." Look at them, beaming at me. I feel like crap for ruining their moment. "So, what happens now?" They look at each other. "I mean, you're just going to stay here, Mom?"

"No, sweetie."

"We haven't worked out the details yet," Uncle Bert says, "but I'm flying back with you tomorrow."

"Oh."

"I'll be staying in a hotel, of course."

"Does everyone else know?" Jeremy asks.

"The lord and lady, you mean? Yes. Can't say your father is overjoyed, but he'll come around."

"What problem does he have with my mom?"

"Oh," he says, "it's nothing to do with Marie."

"Money," Jeremy says. "It's always about money with him."

"Well … it's about the house actually."

Jeremy frowns. "The house?"

"You do know I'm older than your father?"

"Yes, but—oh."

"Oh what?" I say.

"Dovewood House actually belongs to me," Uncle Bert says. "Part of the inheritance."

Out of the corner of my eye, I see Jeremy turn to me, but I keep my face blank. Dovewood House will be my mother's house. Dovewood. My mother. Does that mean she'll be Lady

Marie? I can't let Jeremy know I'm thinking any of that or he'll freak again.

"And you're going to evict them?" Jeremy says.

My mother laughs. "Of course not, dear. We'll have the cottage and Albert's apartment when we're here, and our house in California."

Beaming, Uncle Bert takes her hand. "We'll also be traveling the world, so it makes no sense to disrupt the status quo."

"Right," Jeremy says. "And Chelsea and I should be able to afford our own place soon, Marie."

Uncle Bert leans forward. "That's something else I wanted to talk to you about. Why have you never sent your new banking information to James?"

"James?" I say.

"The family accountant," Jeremy explains and turns back to his uncle. "Why would I do that?"

A mixture of amusement and confusion ripples Uncle Bert's brows. "The trust. He doesn't know what to do with your disbursements."

"I'm sure Dad told him."

At that response, Uncle Bert looks even more perplexed. "What does it have to do with Gordon?"

"Well … I don't know how he feels now, but he was perfectly clear about it September last."

"Clear about what?"

"He disowned me."

Uncle Bert falls back, shaking his head. "Oh, son, you've always taken your father too seriously. Firstly, he's all bark and no bite. Secondly, although he could disown you in his personal affairs, he doesn't have the authority to change the terms of the trust. But, most importantly, he would never disown you in any sense. You mean everything to him."

Jeremy, who had just reached for his wine glass, freezes, staring at it. After a long moment, the corners of his mouth curl a tiny bit. Slowly, he lifts his head, but his eyes keep that faraway look.

"So?" Uncle Bert says. "You'll contact James?"

Jeremy snaps to. "Yes. I will. Definitely."

fifteen

We've been home for three days, but we haven't quite returned to our normal routine. Jeremy's lying on our bed reading when I rush in with the box from the Notting Hill antique shop. "My dress arrived," I tell him.

He puts down his book and watches as I get the outer box open and lift out the inner one. I hesitate for a minute, afraid the dress might have lost some of its magic during the trip from England to California. So much of London seems like a dream already. I look at Jeremy; he motions for me to get on with it. I lift the lid and fold back the tissue paper.

One word whooshes out. "Oh."

Jeremy sits up straighter. "What's wrong?"

I shake my head. "It's everything I remembered." I lift it from the box and hold it in front of me as I walk to the full-length mirror. Jeremy gets up to stand behind me. "Is it too beautiful for me?"

He kisses the top of my head. "Nothing is too beautiful for you."

I roll my eyes.

"Don't," he says.

The tone in his voice draws my eyes to his in the mirror.

"Be gracious," he says. "Accept the gifts I can give you."

"I'm sorry. I didn't—"

"It's roughly one hundred dollars."

I jerk the dress away from me. "My God. How could you pay that much for a dress?"

"No." He takes the dress from me and drapes it across the chair beside us. "Not that. You've wanted to know about the trust disbursement. Annually, it adds up to a more than a hundred thousand."

"Oh no. I didn't give the trust a thought. That's your business."

Up go the brows. "The ink is barely dry on our open and honest agreement, and you—"

"Okay. Yes. I've been wondering." Suddenly, the amount he said sinks in, and my mouth drops open. "You're not serious." Crap. He'll think I'm too excited about the money. "I mean ... whatever."

He shakes his head, smiling. "Whatever?" He wraps his arms around me. "I expected a little more excitement."

I squee for all I'm worth.

"That's more like it."

"We can afford a place of our own now, right?"

"Well ..."

"Not funny, Jeremy."

"Yes. We'll move." He nuzzles my neck.

"Oh, so now I owe you sex?"

He looks at me through the mirror. "You owe me nothing, but I ask you to allow me to give you what small pleasures I can."

I narrow my eyes at him. "Why do I feel like you're testing

dialogue here?" He pretends to be insulted, but he's done that before, so his act doesn't play with me.

"I no longer write romance, remember?"

"But you do want sex."

"Do I?" he whispers in my ear, while slipping his hand under my tee.

His hand is warm and firm and smooth against my skin. His fingers slip into my bra and tease my nipple. I close my eyes.

"Watch," he whispers. And I do. He lifts my shirt over my head and removes my bra. His hands cup my breasts. He braces his feet and takes the weight of my body as I lean against him. "Lift your hair."

He runs the tip of his tongue down my neck and across one shoulder as he massages my breasts with the lightest pressure. I gasp when he clamps my nipples between his fingers. And then he releases them, sliding his hands down to unzip my jeans.

"Open your eyes," he says.

Unaware I'd closed them again, I obey. He spreads his legs wider, lowering his center of gravity, lifting me with his left arm around my waist. My jeans slide down, and I kick them away. His right hand slips into my panties. I hold my breath as his fingers begin their blissful movement. I'm panting when he finally lays me down and gives me almost more pleasure than I can stand—his ultimate "gift" indeed.

Afterward, when we're lying quietly, drifting, he whispers, "Thank you."

I open my eyes, expecting to see his grin. But his eyes are soft, a glint of tears shining. "You're freaking me out," I say. "Are you not telling me something?"

"I love you."

I'm just about to smart off when I remember my conversation with Ethan. Jeremy's not saying those words idly. I brush his hair away from his face and lay my hand on his newly beardless cheek. "And I love you."

♥ ♥ ♥

Jeremy and I have taken a break from work to spend the day with Gabi and Matt. Jeremy, feeling generous with his newly returned wealth, offered to take us somewhere fabulous for lunch, but it's raining, and Gabi's in a mood. So we're at their place eating tacos on TV trays and watching a rugby game. (Matt and Jeremy have a give-and-take on sports.) Well, actually, Gabi's only picking at her food … if that.

"Is B.G. giving you fits today?" I ask her.

"A little." She pushes her food away. Matt reaches over and adds it to his plate.

"I'm going to start a load of laundry." Gabi gets up and leaves the room.

I finish my taco and follow her to their laundry alcove off the kitchen. She's leaning over the washer with her land on her lower back.

"Are you sure you're all right, Gabs?"

She straightens up and starts the water filling. "Yeah. Great."

I watch her add the detergent and stuff the clothes in. Then she shuts the lid and just stands there. Very still.

"This is it, isn't it, Gabs?"

She puts a finger to her lips.

I whisper angrily. "I'm no expert, but I'm pretty sure you can't ignore labor."

She rolls her eyes. "How could I possibly ignore it?"

"I mean you have to tell Matt. You have to go to the hos-pital. Your mom was in labor only three hours with you—start to finish." She stiffens again, concentrating. "Oh wow, that's too close together, Gabi."

She gasps and presses her hand to her crotch. It comes away wet.

I yell for Matt. "Time to go."

Nothing happens for a moment, and then the TV goes silent and two pale-faced men appear in the kitchen.

"For real?" Matt says.

Gabi nods furiously. "Get my stuff."

Matt and Jeremy disappear. With my arm around Gabi, we walk slowly out of the kitchen to the bedroom where I help her change into clean sweats. Jeremy, stunned, is leaning against the wall outside the kitchen. Matt rushes around gath-ering an armload of things. I grab my purse and hoodie from the sofa. Jeremy hasn't moved.

"Come on," I say to him.

His eyes open even wider. "We're going with them?"

"Of course we are. You know I'm one of her coaches."

"Right. I'll drive you there."

"We're all going together."

Gabi hands me her phone as we get into Matt's truck. "Tell Barbara we're on our way."

"Fuck!" Matt pounds the steering wheel. "I forgot to call the midwife."

Gabi's concentrating again, so I say, "Gabi already did. I'm calling her back to tell her we're on our way to the hospital."

Jeremy's staring straight ahead, still doing his deer in the headlights impression. The rain picks up, drumming on the roof, and Matt's driving like a maniac.

"Slow down, Matt, unless you want to skid off the road and deliver this baby in a ditch."

"Oh my God." Jeremy says. "Oh my God."

At the hospital, they whisk Gabi away, so Jeremy and I stay with Matt while he gets her signed in. Jeremy's almost calm until he realizes I expect him to go with me to Gabi's room.

"Not while she's in labor," he says. "I'll wait here."

"The whole point is to be with her through her labor and delivery, Jeremy."

"Right. Go ahead."

"Where has your head been the whole time we've discussed this?" He looks at me like I've just asked him to tell me the population of Jamaica. "None of Matt's family can get here in less than three hours. You are his moral support. It's all of us. Matt, Gabi's mom, me, and you."

"You've gone around the bend. They'd never allow all of us in an operating theater."

I just shake my head and grab his arm, pulling him along. Matt's already out of sight, but Gabi's mom, Chiara, is just arriving when we get to the prep area. She hugs me without really looking at me. "How is she? Is the midwife here? Oh, I'm so nervous."

A nurse exits Gabi's room. She points at me. "You the backup coach?"

"Yes."

"Good because Dad's a little iffy right now."

Jeremy groans.

"She's ready," the nurse says. "All in."

Chiara goes straight to Gabi and kisses her. Matt's sitting in a chair beside the bed, his breathing rapid and his head hung low. Jeremy hasn't moved away from the door. Barbara, the midwife, is already in the room and catches my eye, nodding toward the head of the bed.

I wait behind Chiara until another contraction starts. "Chiara, could you get Jeremy and make him sit down?"

"Oh, certainly. I think I need to sit too."

As soon as her mother moves, I grab Gabi's hand and whisper encouragement to her, watching the fetal monitor for the contraction's peak, then letting her know when it's almost over.

"Going to be a quick delivery," Barbara says. "You want to get on your knees for a while, Gabi?"

Matt comes back to life. "I thought she was supposed to walk around first."

"She did her walking around stage at home," Barbara ells him.

Matt gives Gabi a dark look. "Gabriella, you promised to —"

"Contraction," I announce, and he looks ashamed, but he grabs Gabi's other hand and holds it to his lips. After that he does his job well, using his muscles to help support Gabi on her hands and knees and finally at the squatting bar.

Between contractions, Barbara chats quietly with Chiara, but rarely takes her eyes off Gabi. The nurse comes in and out, consulting with Barbara and getting the warmer ready for the baby. Matt takes photos with his phone, but Gabi forbids him to share any of them online. Jeremy sits quietly, looking anywhere but at the bed.

And then it seems that everything happens at once, and soon I'm choking up at the sound of the baby's first cry. It's a boy. Gabi will have to try again for the daughter she's always dreamed of having. I look for Jeremy and find him on his feet leaning in for a better look, the wonder of it all softening his face so I see the boy captured in the photos on the walls at Dovewood. I don't think he's even registering that the baby he's staring at so intently is breastfeeding.

One Month Later

I'm absolutely split in two. The outside me is aware that Gabi is securing my Juliette cap, and Laura's fastening a bracelet on my wrist, and Mom is fussing because the officiant hasn't arrived yet, and Amanda is fretting that Ethan won't take the ceremony seriously. The inside me is totally freaked.

I'm getting married. Married. Minutes from now. But that's too soon. I'm sure Jeremy and I haven't discussed everything we should have. I'm not prepared enough. Oh God. What if Jeremy's not prepared either? I mean, what do the two of us know about marriage? What do we know about life?

My panic must be visible because Gabi whispers, "Just breathe. You're ready for this."

"Am I?"

Laura holds my hand, leaning in so the three of us are like conspirators. "You simply can't doubt that. You and Jeremy are perfect together."

"What's happening? What are you whispering about?" Mom says. "Is there a problem?"

"No," Gabi says, "just a loose eyelash. All fixed."

Gabi and Laura appeal to me with their eyes. I nod.

"You look beautiful," Gabi tells me.

"So do you ... both of you." I put my arms around their waists, and we squeeze together in front of the mirror.

"Damn," Gabi says. "We are gorgeous."

My brother Scott peeks into the room to announce they're ready for us. Mom kisses me on one cheek and Amanda on the other before they leave with him.

Laura hugs me. "I love you, sister," she says and follows them out.

"Oh shit." Gabi presses her forearms against her breasts. "If I leak through this dress, I'm going to sue the maker of these nursing pads."

A minute later, we sigh with relief when she moves her arms and all is dry.

Ryan who, as my oldest brother, will be walking me down the aisle, opens the door and comes in. Gabi hands me my bouquet, then picks up her bouquet and the card printed with my vows. Ryan offers me his arm, and it seems before I take another breath the three of us are standing behind the shoji screen set up on the patio waiting for the music cues. Gabi's intro begins, and she turns to give me a quick smile before she steps forward.

I'm shaking. Ryan lays his hand over mine. "Does this mean you're a grown-up now, Cheesy?"

"Probably not."

"Sure you are." He kisses my cheek.

The first notes of "A Thousand Years" sound, and an unbelievable calm fills me. Jeremy chose that song for us. For me.

Ryan gives a little tug, and we're on our way. When I step out from behind the screen, the rustle and movement of everyone standing to face me is a distraction. Then I focus on Jeremy and everyone else disappears. It's just the two of us in the first glow of sunset with the air clear and warm and rose-scented. A mondo wave of love washes over me, lifting my heart and rushing it toward him.

And then I'm standing beside him, hearing but not hearing the officiant's opening. Beautiful words like promises and journey and trust float around me. Jeremy's hand finds mine.

"Jeremy and Chelsea," the officiant says, "do you, with your family and friends as witnesses, present yourselves here willingly to be joined in marriage?"

"We do."

"You may now speak your vows."

Gabi hands my card to me. Jeremy and I face each other.

I look into his eyes, and I'm gone. I'm supposed to say my vows first, but I can't do it. I look at the card but can't make sense of the words. Am I having a stroke or something? Panicked, I look up at Jeremy. A brief frown creases his brow, and then he gives a tiny nod and motions to Ethan for his card.

Jeremy clears his throat. "Chelsea Marie Cole, on this most important day, I take you to be my wife. I promise to stay faithfully with you, laugh and cry with you, encourage and grow with you. I promise to love you … to be open and honest …" He pauses, scanning the rest of the card. He shakes his head. He hands his card to the officiant. "I can't do this."

I can't breathe. Oh God.

Gabi leans over my shoulder and hisses, "You asshole. I'm going to murder you."

Jeremy looks at her, surprised. "No, no, I didn't mean …" He takes my hand again. "I just can't say what I wrote." He turns to our guests. "Forgive me for going off script … and for any possible indelicacies I might reveal."

Now my heart is hammering for a different reason—what the hell is he about to reveal?

He faces me again. "I noticed you the first day I moved into Ocean View. Your pink-striped hair caught my eye first and seconds later your beauty—and by instinct, I knew your beauty was not skin deep. I thought surely a woman like you would be unavailable, but when it seemed you were, I resolved to meet you. I practiced clever lines hoping to make an impression the next time I saw you, but each time I looked at you, all words evaporated. Ethan can attest that I told him I'd met the one I wanted to spend the rest of my life with."

Ethan nods.

"And he could also tell you how hilarious he found it that for the first time in the history of my relationships with the opposite sex, I was petrified to make a move."

Ethan grins and nods again.

"And then I heard you crying over the loss of your job, and I thought, Here's my opportunity. I can help this damsel in distress—and yes, I admit I fancied myself your knight, swooping in to rescue you. I brought you pizza and ... well, I acted the bumbling fool, and the evening ended in spilled beer and bloodshed. Yet, I couldn't abandon hope, not even though you blacked my eye and jumped from one wildly wrong conclusion to another and corrected your mother on my sexual preference ... loudly ... in a crowded restaurant. You were a gorgeous, charming, walking disaster, and I was hopelessly in love."

He pauses to blot my tears with his pocket square. "I was also terrified I'd muck things up if I moved too fast. It was torture working with you day after day after day without giv-ing myself away. Good God, it was brutal trying to ignore you lying on my bed in your fu—stilettos. And when you made it clear you weren't looking for a serious relationship, I nearly lost hope. But I gave in, taking your proposal we be only friends with benefits as a do-or-die challenge.

"And I lived. We lived."

He swallows hard, twice. "You are everything to me, Chelsea Marie Cole. I have loved you from that first minute, and it will be my honor and my privilege to love and care for you forever with all my heart and body and soul."

Oh, what a beautiful, beautiful man this is. With sobs and sniffles surrounding me, I'm fighting like crazy not to start full-on boohooing. Then I see Ethan wipe away a tear, and the shock of that kicks my joy into gear.

I toss my vows card. "Jeremy Windsor Pearce, I'm going to love the hell out of you for the rest of your life."

When the laughter stops, the officiant leads us in the exchange of rings. And then we're kissing and everyone's cheering and we're crossing the lawn to the reception tent together as Mr. and Mrs. Pearce.

I can hardly believe I'm standing here beside my husband under the stars in the glow of fairy lights strung in every tree and shrub and crisscrossed over the portable dance floor. If I didn't feel so alive, I'd think this was all a dream. Mom and Uncle Bert look adorable slow dancing together, gazing into each other's eyes. Gordon and Amanda are making the rounds like the social pros they are, speaking with all my friends and relatives. The three prettiest unattached female guests are swarming around Ethan. Of course. I'm betting he won't be going back to his hotel alone tonight. I breathe deeply of all this beauty and peace.

"What the fuck?" Jeremy growls. "She's been with him all evening."

I follow his glare. Laura is deep in conversation with Dusty Haines, ex-surfer pro. "Chill, dude, you won."

"What?"

"You can't possibly still be jealous. You got the girl."

He shoots me a glare. "I was never jealous."

"Seriously?"

"All right. I was. But how can Laura find him at all interesting? She's never surfed in her life."

"Um … could it be that they're both heavily invested in saving the environment?"

"Him?"

"Very much."

"Crap."

I wrap my arms around his waist. "I love it when you talk like me."

"Get a room," Matt says behind me.

I let go of Jeremy and turn to find the happy new family standing there.

"We'd like to dance for a few minutes," Gabi says, laying Marco in Jeremy's arms.

She doesn't fool me. She's lobbying for me and Jeremy to have a baby soon so our children can grow up together. I must admit I feel a pull seeing how natural he looks smiling into Marco's chubby little face.

"He's just nursed and had a diaper change," Matt says, "so you should be good." He pulls Gabi toward the dance floor.

A minute later, Mom, Uncle Bert, Gordon, and Amanda line up before us. "That's a nice sight," Amanda tells Jeremy.

"I agree," Mom says and takes the baby from him.

"Don't rush things," Gordon grumbles. He pulls an envelope from his jacket pocket. "On behalf of the four of us, we'd like you to have a bit of a head start on setting up your household."

"Thank you," Jeremy and I chorus. He takes the envelope

but doesn't open it. I suppose that's proper etiquette, but you know me. I grab it and pull out the check.

"Holy crap."

"Oh, Chelsea," my mother groans, but everyone else laughs, even Gordon.

Uncle Bert holds out another envelope to Jeremy. "Marie tells me Chelsea's never been to Paris, and I know you've already made honeymoon reservations at the"—he looks to Mom—"Pink Palace?"

"Tickled Pink Inn," she says.

He smiles at her like she's just originated that adorable name. "Yes, that's it. So when you get back from Carmel, I'd like you to spend a week abroad as my treat."

Jeremy takes the envelope and pulls me closer to his side. "As a kind and wise and gorgeous woman once said, 'Holy crap.'"

♥

High Tea & Flip-Flops

What could mellow SoCal and high-society London possibly have in common?

Chelsea Cole is only one paycheck away from—OMG—moving back to her mother's house, which would really suck because she's trying to catch the eye of the gorgeous Brit who moved into the apartment above hers.

Jeremy Pearce is definitely not Chelsea's usual blond and bronzed surfer type. He's all sexy long hair, poet shirts, suede boots, and secrets. Lots of secrets. But how will she get close enough to solve the Jeremy puzzle if she keeps humiliating herself every time he's around?

BOOK 3

Open & Honest (Sometimes)

Just when you think you've got it all under control, life happens.

Chelsea Cole Pearce has a Perfect Life Plan: get married, buy a house, and have a baby. Two down, one to go--and she and Jeremy are eagerly working on that third one. (And loving it.) While he's writing his literary novel, she's writing romance and designing her dream nursery. Life in the Pearce household is totally awesome—until it's not. The road to happily ever after is bumpier than Chelsea anticipated, and she's trying not to freak out. But her talent for jumping to wild conclusions coupled with their difficulty being open and honest with each other complicates matters. Now Chelsea must devise a new plan to get their life back on track … or else.

Also by Linda Cassidy Lewis

Edgewater Love Series

Book 1

Building Love

What if he knows her better than she knows herself?

To Brigid Marino, life in Edgewater is fine just the way it is, thank you very much. Why everyone else is excited to see things changing there is beyond her. Sure, it's nice to have new customers discover her family's tavern, but one of them, the mysterious Alex Conner, makes her uneasy.

He's gorgeous and possibly rich—so what? She's made it clear to him that his oh-so-blue eyes and smoky laugh do nothing for her. Yet, he keeps coming back. So …

Game on.

Brigid's determined to uncover Alex's secrets while he wastes time trying to convince her life would be perfect if only she'd see things his way. As if …

Midnight Love

In romance, when opposites attract, it's the differences that make love perfect.

Roxy Ostrowski never dreamed that at thirty she'd have zero love life, be jealous of her BFF, and lose the best job she ever had. Life can only go uphill from here, right?

Wrong. She'd enjoy her new job tending bar in the neighborhood tavern if not for Jack Matthews. Roxy's nicknamed him "Grim" because he never smiles and barely speaks to her no matter how much she tries to charm him. Then one night, Jack reveals he's actually warm and personable. Who knew?

As Roxy gets to know Jack better, she's sure they're becoming more than just friends. So imagine her shock when an unexpected encounter leads her to conclude she couldn't have been more wrong. But why won't her stubborn heart let go of the feeling she and Jack were meant to have a happy ending?

The Bay of Dream Series

Book 1

Spanning ten years, *The Brevity of Roses* explores the interwoven lives of three damaged people who are each offered a chance to heal—if they can banish the ghosts of their pasts.

Meredith Dahlberg-Lang hides behind a façade. In public, she's a wealthy socialite. In private, she's a lonely woman with a heart imprisoned by guilt after her husband's death. But she can't deny the longing she feels when a younger man seeks her attention.

Jalal Vaziri, after years of trying in vain to win his father's approval, defies him by pursuing a new career. When he meets the woman of his dreams, his satisfaction is complete, but fate challenges his plan for a blissful future.

Renee Marshall, matured beyond her years by a hard life, heads for a fresh start in Los Angeles. But when car trouble detours her to a village on the central coast, she enters the life of a man whose fierce denial of the need to be loved matches her own.

Book 2

A poignant exploration of marriage and motherhood, *An Illusion of Trust* is the story of a young woman who discovers that having her dreams come true can't erase her nightmare past.

When Renee Marshall married Jalal Vaziri, she got all the love and security she craved. But now, with a baby on the way, she has to leave her perfect seaside cottage to move into the mansion Jalal shared with his beloved first wife—a woman Renee fears she'll never completely replace. Unsettled by changes the relocation makes to her idyllic life, she allows her dark memories to resurface and feed her insecurity. With the threat of losing all she treasures, Renee will have to confront her past and learn to trust love.

ACKNOWLEDGMENTS

As always, I thank my family for loving, encouraging, and supporting me in many ways. Special mention, and much love, goes to my husband, the man who does far more than his share in real life so I have abundant time to spend in my fictional worlds.

Thank you, Jennifer Neri, for suffering through a thousand emails from me during the writing of this book. Your support was greatly appreciated.

Another thank you goes to my beta readers: Kasie West, Terry Self Parman, Judith Baxter, and Dee Branzell.

And, of course, thank you dear readers. Without you, the story is incomplete.

ABOUT THE AUTHOR

Linda Cassidy Lewis believes life is all about relationships, and her fiction reflects that. She was born and raised in Indiana and now lives with her husband in California where she writes versions of the stories she held in her head during the years their four sons were growing up. She lives in the city and is thankful for the gift of imagination that whisks her away to sea or mountain or countryside whenever she wishes.

Linda loves hearing your thoughts about her books, so please consider leaving a brief review at your favorite bookseller's site. When you visit her website, don't forget to sign up for her newsletter to stay informed about her future book releases.

Website: lindacassidylewis.com
Facebook: http://www.facebook.com/lindacassidylewis